THE DEVIL'S OWN DAY

Cole Swope Coonce

K-Bomb Publishing 2010

THE DEVIL'S OWN DAY

FIRST EDITION 2010

"What the Civil War did to the South is far more extensive than even Southerners know. The statistics are enough to rock you on your heels. The year after the war the State of Mississippi paid a solid fifth of its total income on artificial arms and legs for veterans coming back from the war.

"The hardships of the war you wouldn't even consider nowadays. The absence of nails or needles kept you from mending clothes or keeping the roof from coming off your house. We were without those things, and it had a terrible influence on us... I have great admiration for the way people managed to survive and what they did to survive. What they survived is unimaginable to us. And it had continued through the war and continued after the war, as retaliatory measures were passed against them during the Reconstruction days." – Shelby Foote

Library of Congress Cataloging-in-Publication Data
Cole Coonce, 1961-
THE DEVIL'S OWN DAY / Cole Coonce
ISBN 0-9719977-8-0
1. Deconstruction in the Alleged Post-Reconstruction Age — Meditations on. I Title
Photographs by Cole Coonce, Vasily Suzuki
Art direction, Design, Infotainment scans: Andy Takakjian
KeroseneBomb Publishing
Los Angeles, CA 90041
kerosenebomb.com
Manufactured in the United States of America

PRAISE FOR HERR COONCE

"Aside from his ability to nail down characters without devoting a lot of words to their characterizations, Coonce writes in a fun-to-read energetic, industrial, pre-Apocalyptic fashion. Kind of like a mescaline hangover." —D. Brian Burghart, *Reno News & Review*

"Cole Coonce is a VTEC Tom Wolfe, a literary autojournalist tricked out with nitrous oxide and nightvision, writing for The Fast and the Furious generation."—Adam Fisher, Senior Editor, *WIRED magazine*

"Tonight my butt's got a permanent ring around it after an extended stay in the library, reading Cole Coonce's '(Top Fuel) Wormhole.' Coonce is a Steinbeck/Kerouac/London banana split, and may just earn HOT ROD its first Pulitzer."—Larry Tolle, *HOT ROD Magazine*

"Cole is a writer that has expanded raceminds beyond jetting, performances, indexes and politics. His style has been to explore elements of the acceleration persona that transcend space available in mere magazines."—Phil Elliot, *draglist.com*

"(*Come Down from the Hills & Make My Baby*) is worth picking up for its sexy, nihilistic description of transvestite strippers alone. But as a historical document, it's priceless."—Evan George, *Los Angeles Alternative Press*

"(H)is angst-filled tale is like a beat novel for today's disgruntled youth." —Jonathan Williams. *Prick Magazine.*

BREAD WAS BROKEN WITH:

Kate Petre, Takakjian, Prieboy, Tottenham, NKR, BZ, Dr. Edwin Cole, Krcmar,
Techno Tim, Tony 19, Robert C. Post, Cuz'n Roy, Jack Logan, The Garo Foundation,
Cuz'n Curtis, Sonny, wrenchski, HNR Clark, Bo Fingers
and "Flushright" Florreich's venison-grease biscuits.

ART DIRECTION: ANDY TAKAJIAN
ILLUSTRATIONS & AUTHOR SKETCH: JACK LOGAN
CONFEDERATE DEAD PHOTOS: COLE COONCE

FOREWORD

COONTAIL COLLECTIBLES AND
THE MICROFILM FOR ROMMEL

The oral history about some psychic, cerebral and strategic connection between Nazi Field Marshall Erwin Rommel and Confederate General Nathan Bedford Forrest—how Rommel had thoroughly studied Forrest's Civil War battle tactics to the point of actually retracing his predecessor's steps—collides at the gates of a musky graveyard on the grounds of the Brice's Crossroads battle site. It was there that I began to understand just how pushed, damaged and Jungian the folklore really was. At this junction—an intersection cherished by those who know the minutiae of war history, yet ignored to oblivion by the rest of the world—sat a late model Chevrolet Impala SS sedan sporting Texas plates, parked in front of a rather ramshackle replica of a cannon. Because of the generic make and model of the car, and the fact that it was domestic, it appeared to be a rental. Most probably, some Civil War Moonie had rented the car in his or her hometown and blasted across Texas, Louisiana and the Mississippi delta to get a solitary glimpse of the same battlefield that, legend has it, intrigued Rommel.

As I entered the gates near the graveyard for the confederate dead, I encountered the driver of the rental car. He was some mid-40s, mustachioed Civil War zealot in a Hawaiian shirt, khaki shorts and leather sandals. My presence startled him, but he briskly recovered from the shock of happening upon somebody on a forgotten battlefield to a bug-eyed look that misspoke of a mutual understanding, thinking he had encountered at this, arguably the most esoteric and ignored theater of war in North America, a fellow traveler, another damaged expert on all matters military—a connoisseur of the conquest, an authority on annihilation and an enthusiast of eradication... and a friend of

Forrest… Which wasn't me, but I am not sure I would have corrected him had he inquired to that effect. In his zeal to share, he proffered a beefy paw pinching a roll of 35mm negatives between a saline-swollen forefinger and thrombotic thumb, and for the benefit of my analysis, he said: "I have the micro-film for Rommel." His pronouncement provoked a loud silence. I was stunned. He took my muted response for awestruck appreciation of what he was saying.

"Everybody knows Erwin Rommel came here in the 1930s to study the lay of the land at this, the site of the greatest American Civil War dark horse victories," the Hawaiian shirt explained.

As the Teutonic Tropical Texan put his "micro-film" in the pocket of his garish garment, he concluded, "This time the Germans are going to get it right."

Then he drove off towards Tupelo.

DO FOLKS ACTUALLY COLLECT COONTAILS?

When my Grandma died in 2001, she was to be buried in the same cemetery in Aberdeen, Mississippi that interred Nathan Bedford Forrest's brother. Before her burial, I left the Episcopalian Church where she lay in state and I gathered my cousin to accompany me on a tour of Aberdeen (a town I lived in briefly as a youth—and as a teenage rebel, one I couldn't get away from fast enough). We walked through the downtown area to see what hadn't been usurped by the local Wal-Mart on the outskirts of town. Beyond the machinations of market forces, I also wondered how much of the so-called "New South" and its enlightenment about racial co-existence had taken root there—had rural Mississippi finally followed the societal vicissitudes most of the country had taken for granted a long time ago? During our walk many things were as gothic and languid as they had been twenty years earlier, the last time I had visited the place: For example, the diner was still there—the same lunch counter one of my spinster Aunts had picketed in the 1970s when the restaurateurs had belatedly acknowledged the 1964 Civil Rights Act and finally started seating and serving blacks. The local walk-in movie house was still there—the same bijou that I patronized as a teenager in the 70s and watched actor Joe Don Baker portray Sheriff Buford Pusser in the no-nonsense tale of a Mississippi lawman taking on the moonshine mob with a tire iron, Walking Tall. Back then what struck me as curious was that the movie house was only open on weekends and that the theater owners made Negroes sit in the balcony.

Nowadays the theater is shuttered. My guess is that videotape rentals at Blockbuster had taken care of the actual movie-going experience and had rendered discussions about segregated seating in the local nickelodeon moot.

While the mortuary mongers warm the motors on Grandma's hearse, and after marching up and down the Main Street with my cousin, we take a wider orbit into the residential area that surrounds downtown. This is neither the richest section of town nor the poorest, but here blue and white-collar blacks and whites co-exist on streets where antebellum mansions can be scored for $70,000. Encountering sundry slices of life sipping soda pop and swinging on porches or walking down the street, my cousin and I acknowledge that race relations seems peaceful if not simpatico.

In our travels, I see a sort of Quonset hut turned into a store. The sign outside reads "Coontail Collectibles" and its iconography features a raccoon.

I cannot figure out if the semiotics and semantics of the sign are harmless or an outrageous racist caricature. Do folks actually collect coontails around here? Is that a euphemism?

"C'mon, man," I tell my cousin, pointing at the smiling 'coon. "We have to deal with this place."

WHAT THEY DIDN'T MENTION

The more I study the collectibles store, the more I realize the place is a shrine to Nathan Bedford Forrest. Despite interrupting their lunch hour, the husband-and-wife antebellum memorabilia merchants spend the better part of the afternoon discussing the myths and folklore of the object of their passion, Forrest.

The stories are legion. One tale after another of Forrest risking his own neck in some daring ill-advised personal assault on enemy positions while his inferior forces triumphed exquisitely over a legion of bamboozled Yankees, each battlefield assault punctuated with pithy, percipient yet cornpone punch lines such as "Get there firstest with the mostest," "Never stand and take a charge… charge them too," and "Get 'em skeered and keep the skeer on 'em."

"This Forrest fellow was epic," I tell my Cousin.

"Yes, he was," he agrees, "but these fine folks didn't tell you about all of his exploits."

"Really? What did I miss?"

"What they didn't mention was that after the war Forrest was a charter member of a little post-war Southern social club."

"A post-war social club? What kind of social club? You mean like the Veterans of Foreign Wars?"

"No, it wasn't the VFW."

"What was it?"

"The Ku Klux Klan."

DOBSON'S GRAVE (CSA)

We make our way to my grandmother's place of rest. In a gated section of the cemetery labeled "Confederate Graves," I come across the grave of Civil War general Nathan Bedford Forrest's blacksmith. According to a plaque at the cemetery, the blacksmith, a Negro named George Dobson, was a "free man" who volunteered for duty in the Army of the Confederate States of America.

"There is some shit," I say to my cousin, "that they didn't tell us about in the history books."

THE DEVIL'S OWN DAY

TRANSFORMATION

IN THE FIRST GREAT WAR I was wounded three times and awarded the Iron Cross and that was not enough. Behind enemy lines, the Italians captured most of my staff. I escaped and that was also not enough.

In the 1930s, my country was on the cusp of broad imperialist expansion and my military career was languishing because I refused a post with the then-fledgling Third Reich's General Staff—a secret organization whose very existence was *verboten* according to the terms of the Treaty of Versailles. Instead, I remained an officer on the frontline.

Which posed this problem: There was no frontline. Yet.

I became an instructor. If I were to transcend this military limbo, I knew I needed to study the tactics of military heroes with unmitigated audacity—those who scored outrageous successes not only on the battlefield, but also in the pantheons of public opinion.

Once I had that established, I would publish these strategies as part of my curriculum. I would endear myself to those propagandists who created paragons and legends. I would rise in triumph.

So I did.

THE AIR STINGS OF CELLULOID (1935)

MY RESEARCH BEGAN IN A STROBING SMOKE-FILLED CLASSROOM at the Potsdam War Academy. There, we were a silhouetted quartet of uniformed men who puffed cigarettes and fidgeted, as we watched a screening of D.W. Griffith's *Birth Of A Nation*. The air stung of crackling celluloid. The soot of history slowly melted from the heat of a movie projector's lamp. As the filmstrip sizzled from age and friction, emulsions decayed and nitrates metastasized, mixing with hot balls of dust that floated through the tobacco haze like dirty satellites in space. It burned the nostrils and singed the eyelashes. I put up with the olfactory and chemical unpleasantness; I was looking for a battle plan. My country had a new Chancellor, whose unbridled love for his country was fervent, if not fanatical.

Traditionally, such national pride was a harbinger of an inevitable eventuality: A call to arms. Much had changed since I last shot at people—or more to the point, ordered others to shoot at people—nearly twenty years ago, but I felt there were military lessons to be gleaned from this movie... that the past would help form my future.

In lieu of an orchestra or a proper pipe organ, the soundtrack to the silent film was a perpetual whir of the projector's motor, a clattering grind of mechanical teeth champing on 16mm sprockets interrupted by a smattering of coughs from the assembled military staff.

Schneider, my spindly adjutant, fussed with a flakey phonograph machine. Two of my subordinate staff officers, Burgdorf and Maisel, befuddled by the movie they had been forced to watch—an American film that purported to explain the necessity of the Ku Klux Klan in the Age of Reconstruction—squirmed from boredom. I was also impatient with the movie's plodding plot and maudlin histrionics. I tapped my creased thighs with leather field gloves. "If Goebbels made such shit he would be shot," I said, and the men chortled. This is part of their job, after all: To laugh at my attempts at humor and put up with my idiosyncrasies—including tonight's. The screening was my idea: I commissioned a print of the film because of my interest in Nathan Bedford Forrest, the savage and savvy Confederate General who, after the Civil War, became the Klan's inaugural Imperial Wizard.

"Schneider! The needle!" I called out with brow raised, my frustration with the ponderous, plodding film compounded by the gnawing silences of the malfunctioning phonograph. The lanky adjutant prodded the phonograph, uttered a perfunctory "Jawohl, Lieutenant Rommel" and strains of Wagner's "Die Walküre" jump-started to life.

On the screen, former friends—and now adversarial soldiers—shot at each other with primitive rifles and then a Title Card read: *"On the battlefield. War claims its bitter, useless sacrifice. True to their promise, the chums meet again."*

The scene cut, and Griffith's portrayal of hand-to-hand combat in the American Civil War resumed. A Confederate soldier is shot and drops to terra firma. His "chum" from the North attacks with a fixed bayonet, and just before the inevitable skewering, recognizes his fallen Southern pal, smiles and puts his weapon down.

"Why doesn't he kill him mit der blade?" the steely-eyed, angular and towheaded Maisel asked, his lanky frame bent in a ball of confusion.

"His enemy must be his brother or his cousin, Ich denke," the dough-faced, bulbous Burgdorf replied.

"In war, there is no room for sentimentality," I countered. "Americans lack the instinct necessary for pure, complete domination."

Birth Of A Nation continued in the background: as strings swell, the compassionate boy is shot and falls over his dead friend. Dying, he caresses his chum's lifeless body.

"Der American's last great conquest was maybe manifest destiny," Burgdorf said. "Then they got soft."

"Ja," Maisel nodded. "Maybe nothing was left so they turned on each other."

DISTURBING DISTORTION

AS THE FILM ROLLED, children played onscreen with sheets and scared each other, apparently a eureka moment for the formation of the Klan. This historical distortion was disturbing.

I tapped an immaculate glove, beating the loam out of the leather's earth tone. It felt like the dirt was sticking to the smoke that had attached itself to the lines in my face—lines recently carved from long nights of study and long days of military training. "This film is less than useless. This is not the history I expected at all. Is this not the story of the origins of the Ku Klux Klan? Where is Nathan Bedford Forrest, the 'Wizard of the Saddle'"?

From the stuttering turntable Wagner's "Ride of the Valkyries" pitch-shifted in full song. Onscreen, Ku Klux Klan vigilantes battled a hapless militia of black men.

I rose suddenly and walked towards the projector, grunting with disapproval. Hyper-real superimpositions of Klan footage lit up my face like a crystal night, with two hooded horsemen galloping and holding a cross. The staff officers scrunched their eyes.

"Turn it off!" I fumed and whacked a rostrum with my pointer. Schneider jumped, reached for a light switch and fumbled with the film projector.

"Enough of this buffoonery and propaganda. I am unconcerned with cartoonish portrayals of final solutions." I must admit I was exasperated, I can't explain my impatience, which is somewhat out of character, other than to say I was frustrated with a lack of inspiration as to how to organize our tank divisions for what seemed to be inevitable, if not imminent maneuvers. "In the event of war, our Chancellor is demanding a new and modern approach to battle. I maintain that we will find our answer in the past—specifically, by studying the battle tactics of Nathan Bedford Forrest, the greatest horse soldier in the American Civil War. To know Forrest, I must go to the source," I said, "to Brice's Crossroads, the site of Forrest's greatest triumph and the battlefield where he exercised his infamous pincer movements to the detriment and annihilation of superior Northern forces. Find me a guide, a survivor—somebody who was there."

"Herr Rommel," Burgdorf balked, "that was over sixty years ago. Ist there anybody there who ist even still alive?"

"If not, we shall be guided by ghosts."

HIS GIFT IS ONE OF APPRECIATION

AT AN AIRFIELD draped by the Mississippi state flag and its stars and bars, a small military band played the final strains of "Dixie." It was a farcical lampoon of pomp and circumstance. In the slashing shadows cast from a silver Messerschmitt prop airplane, my adjutant Schneider slovenly sweated and swatted uselessly at insects. It was a grotesque display of inefficiency. Here I was immaculate in jackboots and a crisp National Socialist uniform, representing the Third Reich and trying to appear dignified in the odious humidity. I killed a fly with my baton.

An unctuous man in a double-breasted black three-piece suit fumbled with the contents of an attaché case.

"Lieutenant," he said, "to facilitate your research and with the compliments of the State Department and Mister Henry Ford, and as a token of our appreciation for your newly elected Chancellor—of whom, Mister Ford is an ardent admirer, allow me to present you with Ford Motor Company's latest luxury touring vehicle, the Lincoln Model K sedan."

"*Danke schoen.*"

"And Lieutenant," the unctuous man continued, "as your visit and your research are unofficial, Mister Ford only requests that his token of esteem remains anonymous. His gift is one of appreciation and requires no publicity."

"Of course. But one question."

"Lieutenant?"

"A Lincoln? Named after the emancipator of the Africans?"

"Yes, I suppose so."

"That's a bit ironic isn't it?

"How so?"

"It is my understanding that Herr Ford never really—how you Americans say—'took a cotton to your Mister Lincoln.'"

TOO WET TO PLOW

AS SWASTIKAS FLAPPED above the front fenders, Schneider guided the massive, magnificent black and chrome Lincoln touring sedan through the moist Mississippi delta, down a dusty, desolate two-lane highway flanked by a smattering of cotton along the side of the road and a sign that read Highway 61. I studied maps as Schneider listened to my directions and made the appropriate turns. Our initial destination was the home of one George Dobson, a surviving Confederate soldier who had traveled with Forrest sixty years earlier. In exact accordance with my calculations, we passed a water silo inscribed with the letters: PANTHER BURN. As I put my field glasses to my face I gave directions and told Schneider to apply the brakes. I saw a couple of ancient Negroes drinking and playing music on a dilapidated porch of a rather dreary home that, according to my maps and information, had to be the domicile we sought. It wasn't much of a house; it was merely an aluminum awning leaning against a tin shanty. Under it, an elderly octogenarian man shared a swing with a high-yellow woman, maybe twenty years his junior. She kept cool in a frayed pink polka dot sundress. He wore overalls, a dusty bowler hat and hid his eyes behind a pair of bulbous sunglasses. He played a primitive-looking guitar and blew into a *harmonika* mounted to an odd, unwieldy neck attachment, his music making interspersed with drinks out of a Mason jar as he imbibed a clear substance of what I gathered to be fermented corn syrup. Between sips and notes on his mouth organ, he chewed tobacco and spat into a brass spittoon. As he resumed playing I could only imagine how foul the reeds of his harp might be.

None of this made sense. Maybe I had miscalculated or perhaps the map was wrong. I ordered Schneider to drive on, before we turned around twice, kicking up dust to no avail after finding nothing. We ended up back where we began. This ramshackle shack was the house we sought—but who were these darkies and where was Dobson?

*****

Once again, I instructed Schneider to stop the vehicle and park under a solitary oak tree. With the windows down and my field glasses on, I observed and listened.

"You old, ugly fool!" the woman—I could only assume she was his wife—scolded. "That shine' gwana' clean your plow."

"Ain't nuthin' done kilt me yet," the ancient black man remarked, tipping the flask defiantly.

I was trying to make sense of this peculiar patois.

The Negro set down his guitar, deconstructed the neck apparatus, put away his harp in the breast pocket of his overalls and then dug in a pouch for a fresh chew of tobacco. The Negress reached for his Mason jar. He beat her to it and clutched it tight as a serpent's neck.

"Gawd dammit, woman!" He swatted at the ether. "Now how's you gonna act?"

I must admit I was flummoxed. We were where we needed to be, but no closer to our quarry—George Dobson, veteran of the Confederate States of America. I informed Schneider that, despite the unpleasantness on that porch and as loath as I am to interrupt a domestic dispute, we must drive onto the property and interrogate these people.

He obeyed. Our Lincoln crept closer to the quarrelers, stirring up a brown cloud of dust. The vehicle and the percolating dirt did not perplex the two porch dwellers in the least. We stopped and Schneider cut the engine, but the arguing couple seemed oblivious to our presence. Without any prompting from me and at a loss to any other action, Schneider honked the Lincoln's horn.

"Who these white folks?" The woman cast a suspicious eye at us. "I hain't never see'd their kind befo'."

"I reckon I have," the black man rattled.

"They all looks like Yankees," the Negress riffed. "Or maybe Ku Kluxs... only worsen."

"Hard to believe they's anything worsen than Ku Kluxs... or Yankees," the Negro declared.

"Hard for you to say," the woman hissed. "Seein' as how you broke bread with the head Ku Klux. That man was the Debbil hisself."

"You so full of bull butter, baby. I ain't takin' no cotton to no Debbil or no Ku Klux."

"Don't tell me. Tell it to that statue of Bedford Forrest them white folks put up in Mem'fus. Tell it to your voice inside."

With a momentary break in their dueling jeremiads, crickets and cicadas chirped and my adjutant and I climbed out of our touring car. Fanning herself first around her neck and then between her legs, the Negress asked, "Y'all boys get lost on your way to the cross burnin'?"

"Cross burning?" I was bewildered.

"Don't be studyin' her," the black man declared. "She be a good woman, just born under a bad sign."

She raised up. "I'm 'bout to hit you with a bad sign."

"That'd be the last thing yo' black self hit."

They each reared back to hit one another, in what amounted to a pantomime of mutual bluff. Their actions and hostility made my adjutant anxious and uneasy.

I broke the tension and the stalemate. "Pardon my intrusion, but I am looking for a Mister Dobson—a Mister George Dobson."

"Who' ak'skin'?"

Without breaking eye contact with the Negro, I snapped my fingers toward Schneider, who saluted me and handed me my papers and eyeglasses.

"I am Lieutenant Erwin Rommel. I represent the former Weimar Republic under the Third Reich. This is my adjutant, Corporal Schneider."

"Say! What's that on your neck, Lieutenant?"

"This?" I fondled a medal, awarded to me during the World War. "The Blue Cross ... a token of honor and a symbol of the Teutonic Knights."

"I tole' you they wuz' Ku Klux," the Negress cackled.

"Shut yo' potted meat hole, woman," the colored man fired back, "and let me talk to the man. Now where y'all from?"

"Deutsches Reich."

"Never heard of it."

"Germany. Formerly The Weimar Republic."

He removed his cap, wiped his brown brow and spat, pinging his spittoon.

I put my eyeglass to my papers. "My information states that this house was once the home of George Dobson, a blacksmith who rode with General Nathan Bedford Forrest's cavalry."

"I reckon he hung his hat here once or twice."

"Can you tell me where he 'hangs it' now?"

"Often as not, on top of this ol' black man's nappy head."

"Your... nappy head?"

"Umm hmmm," he nodded.

"You are George Dobson? But you are a black man."

"American by birth... Black by the grace of God."

I realized there was a glaring omission in my documentation and that my intelligence was faulty. Maisel, Burgdorf, Schneider—who had failed me?

"And this here's my daughter Rosa."

"Daughter? I thought she was..." I caught myself, realizing it was impolitic to question a woman's status, and nodded to the coffee-colored woman. "*Fraulein.*"

"Ku Klux."

I ignored the pejorative. "Mr. Dobson, in your American Civil War..."

"You mean what folks around here call the War of Northern Aggression?"

"Yes, yes. Precisely. In your war of ... *Northern Aggression*, you rode with Forrest's cavalry from Fort Donelson to Brice's Crossroads. You shod his horses."

"Fort Donelson. Shiloh. Chickamauga. Okolona. Fort Pillow," Dobson said. "Yes suh, I shoed the man's horses all the way to Nashville. Sho' nuff did. That is, when they weren't being shot out from under that crazy sum'bitch."

"I don't suppose one could get any closer to a cavalryman."

"I reckon not."

"And you were at the site of his greatest triumph."

"His greatest?" wondered Dobson.

"Brice's Crossroads, of course."

"He was there, oh yeah," Rosa interrupted. "Sho' 'nuff wuz. Volunteered to clean up the horseshit in all dem' battles—'stead of tellin' the white man to clean up his own horseshit."

"Even an ol' horse don't nag like yo' damn self," Old Dobson seethed.

Ignoring Rosa again, I asked: "I knew that you served under General Forrest, but you volunteered for the Rebels? Why would a Negro volunteer for the Confederacy?"

"We all gots to do what we gots to do to get by," Dobson volunteered.

"Yes, yes, I suppose we do. And in 'getting by,' you became very close to Forrest in a personal capacity."

"Like I said: I shoed the man's horses. Occasionally, I made sho' Massah' Forrest kept his shit together. I was in his service... and I was his... companion."

This revelation perplexed my adjutant. "An Aryan freunde mit undt black mensch...like Huck Finn and Nigger Jim?"

"Boy!" Old Dobson fired off. "You see 'Nigger Jim,' you better give him more than forty acres and a mule. Maybe throw in a white woman. Until then, you show a little respect for this old black man who fought for the Confederate States."

"That's right Pappy!" Rosa hollered. "Don't take no mess from dem' Ku Kluxs!"

"Please, enough of this," I pled, exasperated. "Mr. Dobson, what interests me is what happened at the battle of Brice's Crossroads. You are perhaps the last surviving witness."

"There weren't all that many survivors left after the shootin' stopped," Dobson muttered.

"Mr. Dobson, I want you to tell me about General Forrest's techniques. I am fascinated by the man they called the 'Wizard of the Saddle.'"

"Look man, what in the hell you wanna visit all dem old ghosts for? What's done is done. Besides, like the book say, tomorruh' be another day, ain't it?"

"Yes, yes, what is done is done and tomorrow is another day and other American platitudes, *ad infinitum*." I caught myself starting to become confrontational, which was counterproductive. "I'm sorry. I don't mean to be argumentative. But we must revisit what has happened as the past will inform our future, will it not?"

"The future ain't much of my concern," Old Dobson nodded. "Neither is the past. Any more, I don't see one day bein' all that different from the rest."

*****

Before we left Germany for the Deep South of the United States, I was well-aware that my potential tour guide would be a cranky, antediluvian sourpuss who would try my patience—assuming I could even convince him to help us. But I was not prepared to meet a man of African descent and this surprising turn of events unnerved me, psychologically. His race meant nothing to me in a prejudicial sense, and was only a factor in our dealings because I knew he had no reason to help anybody of the Caucasian persuasion. If my mission was to be successful, I needed to secure his trust—or maybe, just gain his empathy.

*****

I tapped my baton. "Sir, I come in all humility and in need of personal favors. We need an escort to Brice's Crossroads. Your company and guidance would mean a great deal to me."

"I don't know what I can tell you, Lieutenant. That was a long time ago and the melon is gettin' kinda soft."

Rosa made it clear she thought this was less than factually accurate.

"Yo' head hard, not soft," she said, and knocked off his cap.

Old Dobson raised an open palm and shook a fist. "Jeezus, Mary and Joseph. Maybe I will go down the road a piece if'n it means I don't have to listen to this shit fo' awhile."

Dobson took a pull from his flask. Sensing an accord, I set my papers and eyeglasses on the roof of the car and walked towards the porch.

"Perhaps if you were there again," I said, "the memories would not be so... soft. We can chauffeur you to the site of Brice's Crossroads and Forrest's famous pincer movement. You can show me everything: The Northern positions, the Confederate positions, everything... from the beginning."

"What kinda' automobile you got?" Dobson asked. "That look like a Ford, sho' ain't no Model T."

"This is a seven-passenger Lincoln. Named after the man who died for your freedom, apparently."

"Ain't nobody ever died for this ol' black man and I hesitate to call myself free," Dobson spat. "You either. But that is one mighty fine sedan."

"Yes," I replied. "Occasionally the Americans get it right."

"'ccasionally."

"Yes, yes, Mr. Dobson. Why don't you accompany me? Take a pleasurable ride with us in this ostentatious example of quaint engineering? You can ride in the back with me."

"I tell you what, Mistah'..."

"Rommel. Herr Erwin Rommel."

"Yes suh', Mister Herr Erwin Rommel. It's a long ride to the crossroads. I reckon I'm gonna need some foldin' money. You wanna get me in that car and have me show you how Forrest whupped up on the Fed'ral troops. Take a nice long ride in a sweet piece of machin'ry. My memory probably get a whole lot better wif some Moon Pies in my stomach."

"*Jawohl.* How many 'Moon Pies'?"

"I reckon one-thousand moon pies will make this ol' black man fat and happy."

"Herr Dobson, understand that our fact-finding mission is one of delicate diplomacy. These Moon Pies will keep you quiet as well as fed?"

"Black folks used to ain't sayin' shit," Dobson said to Schneider. "Particularly with they mouth full."

I felt that Mister Dobson was being somewhat disingenuous. According to what I had read and had gleaned from the cinematic excesses of D. W. Griffith, yes, the Negro population of the Deep South was often a laconic people who tended to avoid trouble. Even after being granted a certain emancipation as a result of the American Civil War, these new citizens learned that this freedom was constantly fraught with challenges and with terror. So the Negroes remained subdued and in the parlance, "knew their place." But Dobson was different—if his exchanges with my adjutant and myself were emblematic, he was bold, blunt and most impertinent with Caucasians. Was this because he felt untouchable, indifferent, or did he welcome the inevitable fatal result of his insolence? He might think that, owing to his advanced age, he was—if I may resort to the local vernacular again—above kowtowing to "Mister Charlie". Further to that, perhaps he felt that since he had served under—and outlived—the military figure that became an integral figure in the formation of the Ku Klux Klan during the beginning of the Reconstruction Era, what harm could come to him at this point in his life? If neither Nathan Bedford Forrest nor the Klan had killed him at this point, who possibly could?

"So Herr Dobson," I said. "We can compensate you for your services with five hundred U.S. dollars, I mean *moon pies* now and five hundred more upon our return. Is that a deal?"

"I reckon so. I cain't dance no' mo' and the fields are too wet to plow."

Both Schneider and I looked puzzled. The terra firma under our feet was, in fact, rather dry. Because we were not familiar with our host's peculiar turn of phrase, we weren't quite comprehending that Dobson had agreed to go with us. But Rosa understood.

"Pappy, don' get in dat' car with those crazy ass white folks. You too fuckin' ol'."

"Hush up, woman, I ain't too ol'…"

Dobson hoisted himself off his chair with some difficulty.

"You crazy-ass fool," Rosa said, helping the old man out of his chair. "Whatchu' think you doin'?"

"Sometimes you just gotta go down the road, woman," Dobson explained to his daughter. "And that's a mighty fine automobile. Now help me fetch my shit."

"You fetch yo' own shit. You takin' blood money again from the white man."

"Schneider," I said. "Take five one hundred dollar bills and present them to Mister Dobson."

"Let my daughter hold it."

The deal was sealed. The creaking screen door closed behind Rosa. In the silence, Schneider stubbed out his cigarette with his jackboots, and stared down at the parched, coffee-colored clay of Mississippi, waiting for Dobson to maneuver his way into the sedan's back seat. Presently, I joined him there.

Rosa watched the Lincoln motor start and then yelled at her father: "You know nuthin' good ever comes from goin' down the road wif white folks."

I AIN'T PLAYIN' SHIT

THE EXHAUST OF OUR QUICK DEPARTURE muffled Rosa's last comment. We barely heard it. I asked our newly-hired guide what his daughter meant by that statement: What was the peril of traveling with my adjutant and myself; we were tourists on a fact-finding trip, and although we were white men, at least we were ones who had no interest in perpetuating the servitude of Africans in America.

Reconstruction was ending. War was over, I told him, and we were not like the others. Perhaps I was being naive about our appearance and how it would resonate with a black man hoping to get through the *dämmerung* of his life without any further racial turmoil or complications. To that end, the Negro endeavored to share an anecdote of antebellum times in Hernando, Mississippi, a few years before the War Between the States. In this story, a large horse-drawn carriage was stuck in a morass of mud, its back wheel fixed in a large puddle, as swamp water seeped through its doors and into the floorboards. In the coach, two white women—the Widow Montgomery, a solemn, older Southern lady, and her daughter Mary, a young, pious, modest and fetching brunette belle— tried to maintain calm as their surroundings became grim. Adjacent to the mud hole, but under the comfort and shade of a massive magnolia tree, two drunken, bellicose upper-crust ruffians had cornered the wagon's driver, a Negro youth, to the tree and taken turns menacing him with his own buggy whip. According to Herr Dobson, as they pushed the youth backwards into the magnolia, one of them snatched a *harmonika* out of the black boy's shirt.

*****

"Hey cracker! Gimme back my harp."

"Boy, I hope you can play this ol' harmonica better than you can drive a horse and carriage."

"I says give it back."

The ruffian tossed the instrument to his buddy and the two young white men began a game of keep-away.

"Why? You want to play us a song?" one of the drunken ruffians asked, tossing the harp to his companion.

"Yeah black boy, play us a song," the other drunk teased.

"I wouldn't play 'Da Camptown Races' at y'all's greasy granny's funeral."

The first drunk dropped the harp and landed a punishing blow to the Negro's face, sending him sprawling. The women gasped.

"Boy, you leave my granny out of this," the second drunk warned.

As the black boy attempted to collect himself, the first hooligan stuffed the harmonica into the boy's mouth.

"You gotta mouth on you, boy. I reckon yer gonna hafta to use it the way society intended. Now go on and play for us, boy."

"I ain't playin' shit."

"I reckon you will."

"Fuck you. I'm free, same as you," the youth responded, and dropped the harp.

At that, both white men began pummeling the hapless carriage driver. Coughing, the black boy held his stomach, as one of the drunks picked up the harp.

"I got a song in my heart, black boy. Listen to this," said the second drunk and while the first ruffian played the harp, the other sang: *"A dog, a nigger, an' a magnolia tree/Th' more yeh beat 'em, th' better they be!"*

The ruffians whipped and whistled at the distressed Negro while the Widow Montgomery issued impotent threats from the carriage. Her daughter Mary sat silently next to her, docile and frightened, consulting her King James Bible for comfort.

"Stop this violence and give our driver back his harmonica, you vandals," the Widow demanded.

She was ignored. The men placed the harp in the black boy's mouth and hit him as he grunted and wheezed through the instrument's reeds. The first ruffian stuck one hand down the front of his shirt and giggled, "Boy, you can't play for pig shit."

"Hush yo' mouth," the Negro gasped. "You dandied-up piece of white trash."

"And you drive worse than you play, steering yer' owners carriage into a crick," laughed the second ruffian. "Whatsamatter? You blind in one eye and cain't see out of the other?"

"Kiss my black ass, soda cracker."

As the menacing began to reach a boil, Mary Montgomery buried her face in her Bible and murmured bits of Ezekiel: *"And mine eyes shall not spare, neither will I have pity; I will bring upon thee according to thy ways, and thine abominations shall be in the midst of thee; and ye shall know that I the Lord do smite."*

Wielding a knife, the second ruffian smacked the Negro across the mouth. "I'll learn you to sass a white man. You'll do his bidding and play him a song."

"To hear that young miss tell it," the first ruffian joined in, "the Good Book says we is to smite the nigger's eye..."

The Widow Montgomery was apoplectic. "You ill-mannered heathens!" she spluttered. "Unhand our driver!"

Mary Montgomery continued reading from the Bible, with more fervor, louder and faster, reciting: *"Violence has grown into a rod of wickedness... None of them shall remain, none of their people, none of their wealth, nor anything eminent among them."*

The second ruffian slit the Negro's eye. He screamed and kicked and the ruffians guffawed.

*****

Then I get my first taste of what I have traveled from the Fatherland to the benighted hinterlands of America to hear. The Old Negro tells that amidst the terror, at a break in the trees, a gallant horseman—a tall and handsome man, dressed in fine but practical riding clothes—stood up in the saddle of his impressive mare and galloped toward the scene. Quick as lightning, he dismounted, nodded to the ladies and pulled a pistol.

*****

Pointing his gun at the second ruffian, the Horseman demanded: "Release that man, you high-and-mighty sot."

"Who the hell are you to tell me what to do?" the second ruffian shouted. "I'm free, white and damn near 21."

"Drop the gun you sonofabitch or he'll cut you too," the first ruffian countered.

The Horseman shot the second ruffian in the hand, knocking the knife into orbit. During the chaos, the carriage driver—although still tied-up—deftly kicked the first ruffian in the groin. The gunshot spooked the horses and they pulled unexpectedly, turning the wheels of the wagon but only digging the carriage deeper into the creek bed, splattering the ruffians with mud and gunk.

Cleaning his face with a handkerchief, the Horseman shouted, "Obviously you ignorant drunks are still too wet behind the ears to know not to bring a knife to a gunfight."

The mud-splattered ruffians and the driver all writhed in agony, covering sundry, maimed body parts. While raising the pistol menacingly, the Horseman wiped much of the mud from his face, standing up straight to look the ruffians in the eye, turned his face without losing eye contact and spat.

"Mister," the first ruffian yelled while running with his back turned, "you are one deranged sonofabitch."

Mounting up, the second ruffian waved and said, "I'll see you again, you bastard."

"In hell's half acre, son," the Horseman laughed. "In hell's half acre."

The first ruffian slipped and fell into the mud. The second ruffian fought for control of his horse with his good hand, and galloped away cursing. The first ruffian got up from the mud and ran after his horse, which trotted off into the forest. All the while, the Negro carriage driver moaned.

The Samaritan threw his horse's rein over a tree branch and walked into the mud and mire, gathered logs and sticks, and placed the wood under the wheels of the carriage. While he worked, he presented himself to the passengers.

"Ma'am, is that your slave?" he asked.

Overhearing the query, the driver covered his eye and muttered in pain, "crazy fuckin' white folks."

"No sir, this Negro is nobody's Negro," The Widow Montgomery responded. "We are God-fearing folks who do not believe in chains of bondage. He is a freeman, and is in our modest employ as a chauffeur and stable boy."

"Ma'am, I am Nathan Bedford Forrest. The auctioning of slaves is my business. You have a good nigger here. Although rather mouthy for his race, the man is brave."

"Lawd Jesus," the maimed Negro groaned. "Nathan Bedford Forrest. Save me from my oppressors… and from my motherfuckin' liberators too."

Oblivious to the driver's suffering, Forrest told the Widow, "If you ever feel the need to sell your property, I do hope you will call upon me."

"I don't think I explained myself properly," the Widow replied. "Mister Forrest, this man is free. He is not ours to sell. He is not anybody's to sell."

"All the same, Ma'am…."

Forrest then took the opportunity to address Miss Mary Montgomery: "In deference to your appreciation of the scriptures, missus, may I say that this afternoon's exchange weren't exactly an eye for an eye, but that hooligan's losing the use of his hand will have to suffice."

Mary bowed her head chastely, flushed and embarrassed from both the excitement and the personal attention. As Forrest mounted his horse, the two exchanged amorous glances. Forrest eyed her as if the seed had already been sown.

Forrest commandeered the horse's reins, and manipulated the animals to rock the carriage forwards and backwards. The passengers swayed with the carriage.

Mary attempted to gather her composure at the end of such a brutal afternoon. "Mother," she whispered, "I feel faint."

*****

So said Old Dobson in the back seat of our touring sedan.

A CHIVALROUS ANACHRONISM
AND A SCHWARZ

AS THE LINCOLN PASSED a grim panorama of agrarian destitution—rusted, corrugated grain silos, disheveled tin shacks, and sweaty black farm hands picking cotton—I found myself basking in Ol' Dobson's account of Forrest's altruism, vigilance and virtue. Having finished this telling of what I took to be his first encounter with Nathan Bedford Forrest, the Negro reached into his breast pocket, retrieved his harmonika and broke into a warbling instrumental. I tried to discourage his playing while rekindling his memories.

"Ahhh, a fine story, Herr Dobson. Your Forrest was a chivalrous anachronism," I marveled, while trying not to wince at the sour notes. "St. George in the dark forest, a gentleman and a soldier!"

"I reckon," Ol' Dobson replied, removing the harp from his mouth.

"He was following his own code of honor."

"Color' folks sho' had another word for it."

"Which was vas?"

"Bugfuck."

"Bug... ficken?" Schneider queried.

"Bugfuck," Dobson confirmed. "The more I knowed him, the more I knowed that sum'bitch was crazy. Putting himself in harm's way became a habit. I ain't sayin' he didn't do right by the Montgomerys, but comes to find out there was always the potential for the man to come unhinged."

"*Non compos mentis*, perhaps, Herr Dobson. But wouldn't you say his dementia was balanced by a peculiar ethos? The man was a slave trader—a trafficker of flesh—yet despite his occupation of dubious propriety, you tell me he came to the aid of a black man in distress. Perhaps Forrest was more sentimental than I gave him credit for."

"The man has been called a whole lotta' things," Dobson said, "but this be the first time I heard him called sentimenta'."

He spat and drank from his flask.

"I understand rescuing der *fraus*," Schneider interjected, turning his head towards the back seat of the sedan. "But why would anybody come to der aid of somebody's *schwarz*?"

"*Schwarz*? Boy, who the hell you callin' *schwarz*?" Dobson took off his sunglasses to reveal his left eye sewn shut. The Negro reared back as if to hit my Adjutant with his glasses.

"Schneider!" I barked. "I know there is not much in front of us, but keep all discourse to a minimum and concentrate on the road ahead. I'll ask the questions."

"*Jawohl.*"

Schneider did not comprehend that while telling the story of Forrest coming to the rescue, Herr Dobson was referring to himself as the young carriage driver, blinded in one eye due to an assault from a pair of ne'er-do-wells. Schneider has always been loyal, but never a *mensch* with much of an intellect.

"Herr Dobson, allow me to apologize for the impertinence of my adjutant."

"Hey man, fuck you too. Likes you give a hoot in hell about hurtin' the pride of some used-up old darkie. Like any other soda cracker, you are here to see what you can get out of the black man."

Dobson took out his mouth organ, licked his lips and played a few notes of a primitive, diatonic scale and began to sing: *"I was free, black and seventeen/But white folks trash made for a very bad scene/Why cain't you let a black man cry?/Tears ain't enough, now there's blood in my eye."*

Between the singing and somewhat flatulent harmonika playing, an awkward silence permeated the motorcar. We continued down the highway against a tableau of poor black field hands bent over in the Mississippi sun, while the fender-mounted flags flapped and fluttered. Treading lightly on account of his delicate mental state, I asked our passenger for more details about how his life became intertwined with that of one Nathan Bedford Forrest. In point of fact, the heroic encounter at the creek bed led to other engagements.

As we continued our sojourn towards the cross roads, in his own inimitable manner, the Old Negro recalled the events from both memory and hearsay.

NEW FACE IN HELL

DOBSON TOLD ME THAT WEEKS AFTER THE ASSAULT and rescue, he observed Forrest in the Montgomery's parlor, enjoining the Reverend Samuel Montgomery Cowan for his niece's—Mary Montgomery's—hand in marriage.

*****

"Why Bedford, I couldn't consent," Reverend Cowan admonished. "This is a most pious family. You cuss and gamble like a river rat and Mary Ann is a Christian girl."

"I know," Forrest said. "That's why I want her. It's my hope that she's pious enough for the both of us. Goddammit Reverend, without our union, there's likely to be a new face in hell."

"Mr. Forrest, that is hardly a ringing endorsement."

"Look at it another way," Forrest reasoned. "The Montgomerys are used to living in a certain fashion. But with the loss of the father, the family's ship has lost its rudder. Because of my fortune and my stature as a self-made millionaire, I can make sure that Mary will live in continued luxury."

"With wealth accumulated by the trading of human flesh," Reverend Cowan retorted.

"Sir, you are a man of the good book," Forrest replied. "You know that in Leviticus the Bible says: 'Your male and female slaves are to come from the nations around you; from them you may buy slaves.'

"What are you trying to tell me, Bedford?"

"Reverend, I am just here doing the Lord's work."

HER ATTRIBUTES

ONE DAY IN 1859 IN THE CITY OF MEMPHIS, TENNESSEE Dobson chauffeured the Widow Montgomery into town for her fortnightly shopping expedition. To their mutual disgust, they encountered the beginnings of a slave auction. In it, two groups of Negroes, segregated by sex, stood on either side of the courtyard. They were smartly dressed, with hats, coats and shoes for the men, and frocks and hair-handkerchiefs for the women. An American flag hung in the background next to a platform, flanked by a medium-sized bureau with inkstand. Despite a madding chatter among the buyers, the slaves kept quiet. To the Widow Montgomery's further dismay, she caught sight of her new son-in-law, Bedford Forrest, looking distinguished, directing the inquiries of a half-dozen older white gentlemen perusing the chattel.

There Mr. Simon Flogg, a small, older pot-bellied plantation owner with a cane, peered at Catharine, a statuesque, light-skinned Negress. Mr. Flogg pulled her lips back with a gloved hand, as if inspecting the teeth on a horse.

*****

"Mr. Flogg, this is Catharine," Forrest enjoined. "You'll want to bid on this fine quadroon. She cooks and cleans and slops the hogs and is smart as a whip—so you'll want to keep her close. I myself have used her both out in the field and in my own home. I'd keep her myself, but the missus says we got too many females already. Her bidding starts at one thousand US dollars."

Mr. Flogg continued scrutinizing Catharine. She did not move under his gaze as he reached out and pulled her chin up to look at her smooth face. He looked impressed but shook his head.

"Mr. Forrest, this is a prime piece of merchandise but you are asking for too much money. She's rather skinny for the shekels you are seeking."

"Too thin? This is an auction, man! You ain't paying by the pound," Forrest responded. "My advice is that you bid something—unless you can get your wife to slop your hogs and pick your cotton."

Flogg tilted his head, eyeballed Catharine's cleavage lasciviously and then palmed her bosom. She sighed under her breath, impatient with the charade. "Oh Mr. Forrest, this one is not to be wasted on picking cotton. Yes, yes, she is a fine but slender specimen. I have a house in New Orleans that could put her qualities to fine and profitable use. A thousand to start the bidding, you say?"

Forrest nodded.

"Mister Forrest, can you show me her attributes?"

"Begging my pardon, ma'am," Forrest said, as he reached in to remove her frock.

Fussily, Catharine pushed his hand away and said, "I can do it myself, suh'."

Forrest backed away, momentarily, and then leaned into her. She pushed him back. Startled, he reflexively raised and cocked the back of his taut, powerful hand. She didn't flinch.

"My, she is high-spirited," Flogg chuckled. "How do you tame such insolence, Bedford?"

"Since you seem so interested in opening the bidding on this woman, I leave that discipline to you," Forrest said and bowed with a theatrical flourish. "Please sir, be my guest. I only ask you do not leave a mark on the merchandise."

Taking his cue, Flogg deftly slapped the woman's face.

She stared, then resumed undressing.

In the distance, the Widow Montgomery implored Young Dobson to drive her back home.

"Yessum," he nodded, looking over his shoulder at the slave woman as she disrobed.

MAN SHOULD KNOW HIS PLACE

"I CANNOT CONDONE SUCH VIOLENCE, NECESSARILY," I reasoned, interrupting the Negro's seventy-year old recollection of the slave auction. "But despite this troubling scenario, I must say that Forrest's ability for establishing a social hierarchy certainly lends itself to his being a military leader. It is a question of knowing one's place—wouldn't you agree, Herr Dobson?"

Dobson spat and wiped his mouth.

"Well, black man," Schneider cut in. "Don't you think that every man should know his place?"

"Motherfucker, I believes I done earned the title 'Mister Black Man.'"

"Schneider! Scheiße!" I was livid. "I command you to show our tour guide more respect."

My adjutant quietly acknowledged his error, saying to Dobson, " Ich bin sorry."

Order restored, I told our guest that—based on my studies of Kierkegaard—I often had existential questions about "place" and "social order."

"It mus' be hard fo' you, Herr Mister Rommel—to be in such a place as to have to worry about the place of others."

"And in your opinion, what is my place?"

"I believes that all mens—white, black or quadroon—are born in shackles," Dobson answered. "That be your place: In shackles. Whether he be in out-and-out bondage, wearing irons after picking cotton, or wearing a uniform and jus' driving an ol', tired black man across the Mississippi delta. It's bondage, jus' the same."

Then he spat out of the window and told me more about that day at the slave auction.

FORGET THE PUBLIC DEBASEMENT

WITH HIS HEAD SWIVELED AND LOOKING BACK, Dobson began to wrangle his wagon away from the town center. But his carriage's progress was halted by civil unrest.

*****

Catharine was naked now. At the auctioneer's prompting she turned and performed a running and jumping routine around the courtyard. Flogg chortled and leered in approval. The more dehumanizing Catharine's stunts, the louder he laughed and the bigger his belly bounced. He playfully poked Forrest with a wad of cash and pointed his cane at the goods. Forrest nodded, his countenance otherwise inscrutable. Then he scowled, sensing discord just beyond the confines of the business at hand.

Indeed, scores of angry, shouting citizens moved towards the town center. The commotion drew closer, a ferocious wave of humanity that spooked Dobson's horses and muted the merriment.

"Thar's gonna be a hangin'!" one of the town's people yelled. "Thar's gonna be a hangin'!"

"This ol' boy done kilt his cousin," yelped another.

The lynch mob dragged a disheveled, gaunt teen to the gallows outside of the courthouse. The accused boy had been tarred and feathered and stood on the gallows shaking. A stream of urine collected around his bare feet.

Forrest shoved a startled Flogg out of his way and gathered his property, handing Catharine her frock. "Get dressed," he said. "I think our business here is done."

The rabble grew like a toadstool. On the perimeter of the disruption, Dobson and the Widow Montgomery were caught in the commotion and rendered immobile by the mass of irate citizenry. Transfixed, they watched Forrest, who was pulling his slave woman by the wrists. Forrest pushed his way through the tumult, towards the gallows. He let go of Catharine, climbed the steps of the scaffold and stood next to a fat, mustachioed man who had raised his short arms and was pleading for judicial procedure. His call for calm was shouted down by the bloodthirsty mob. The man was the Mayor of Memphis, but his official status was moot, having lost control of the citizens of his city. Panic was in his eyes and his chubby hand grasped Forrest's arm.

Forrest shook his head and brushed the portly man off.

The pandemonium continued in the Memphis gallows.

"Let's git this thing done, nah'!" A man brandishing a rope shouted.

Mortified, the Mayor hollered to Forrest, "These animals are gonna lynch a scoundrel who ain't even had a proper trial."

"Sir," Forrest advised, "It is your duty as mayor to stop this and rescue that boy."

Catatonic with fear, the Mayor wagged his double chin in the affirmative.

"You can jiggle your fat face until the cows come home," Forrest warned, "but nothing is going to get done unless you do it. Sir, is it not your duty to save that boy?"

"Oh, it is son," the Mayor acknowledged. "But the fear has gotten the better of duty."

"Ahhh, horseshit," Forrest muttered.

Forrest walked purposefully up to the gallows and with a strong, quick strike with his knife, cut the accused free. Still brandishing the blade, Forrest dragged the teenager under his shoulder, extended a forearm, and muscled his way through the masses as they gradually became aware of what had happened. The roar of the crowd crescendoed, enveloping Forrest as he made his way to the jail. He pushed the accused teen through the hoosegow's open door and stood in the doorway alone, sheathing his large dagger halfway into the crotch of his pants. Then, palming two six-shooters, he faced the hellbent horde and wordlessly dared it to consummate its attack.

"Now, Bedford Forrest," a man in the crowd slurred, "we're not looking to fight you, Sir. We just want that murderin' boy. Justice be done."

"I'll tell you this," Forrest replied. "I'm sure as hell not givin' this boy over to a bunch of half-cocked polecats, no matter what he's done. If you come by ones, or by tens, or by hundreds, I'll kill any man who tries to take over this jail. Such is the justice of this world."

The mob murmured and moaned and began to disperse. Outnumbered and out-armed, the fearless Forrest stared down and quieted the bloodthirsty rabble in the streets of Memphis.

In the shadows of the gallows, Catharine rubbed her wrists and lowered her head in modesty. Her face was flush.

Young Dobson squinted his eyes, surveying the aftermath of a slave auction upended by a riotous lynch mob. Forrest's brazen display of bravery in the face of an overwhelming show of force was formidable all right— even the slave trader's own Negress appeared in awe of her owner's valor and seemed to forget the public debasement and humiliation he had put her through, mere moments before the sale turned violent. Dobson shook his head and spit.

"Mr. Dobson, drive on," the Widow Montgomery implored. "And please refrain from that bilious spitting in my presence."

"Yessum."

BY ANY MEANS NECESSARY

"HE WAS CORRECT, WE MUST HAVE ORDER or we have nothing," I reflected as our Lincoln proceeded down the road in the sweltering Mississippi heat and the octogenarian Negro slobbered once again into his harmonica.

"I reckon Ol' Forrest got order by any means necessary," Dobson mused as coda to his story about Forrest and the vigilantes. "You could say that Forrest wuz' tryin' to make sense of right and wrong like most everybody else. Some say wit' mixed results."

"Mob rule is an example of how allowing the common man a voice is often a mistake," I concluded. "Is that how Forrest felt about American notions of democracy?"

"But if that man felt sump'n," Dobson answered, "he felt it down to his toenails. When he gots a notion, there was always more doing and less thinkin'."

"The right man is the man who seizes the moment," I reflected.

"What?"

"I was merely quoting Johann Wolfgang von Goethe."

The old Negro spat. "Thought so," he said.

BRINGING IN THE SHEAVES

AS OUR PASSENGER PASSED THE TIME by belching into his harp, he hit upon a fragmented variation of a melody I recognized from some of the more pious American soldiers whom I had taken prisoner in 1918 at Verdun. In my memory, it has a refrain of "We'll all go rejoicing," and I asked Dobson if he was playing a hymn. He confirmed my conjecture. He said that all of our talk of Forrest's chivalry, matrimony and slave-trading, as well as his strong sense of defending certain principles, reminded him of an anecdote he heard about Forrest as war began to break out.

It began in a simple but elegantly decorated sitting room, as Mary Forrest (nee Montgomery) sat in an overstuffed upholstered chair, knitting and sort of half-humming and half-singing "Bringing In The Sheaves." A porcine animal howled, startling Mary, who stopped knitting and humming.

In the slave quarters, Forrest and Catharine were in primal yet muted vertical sexual congress. Bent over with one hand on her mouth, and another on her breast, Forrest lunged his hips upward, as if his manhood were a saber. While covering Catharine's mouth with his hands, he reached a brief yet intense climax. It was unclear what physical sensations affected Catharine, as her inscrutable countenance projected anything from pleasure to resentment.

Mary continued humming and resumed her work, crocheting a confederate battle flag for her husband to use in the war that has broken out between the Northern and Southern United States.

*****

At this point in the telling of his story, the old black man resumed playing the hymn on his harp. Then he told me of life during wartime, when United States General William "Tecumseh" Sherman first visited the Confederate States of America and the Montgomery household. According to Dobson, that day was one of indiscriminate pillaging.

BARBARIANS AT THE GATE

AS BLUE-BELLIED SOLDIERS ATTEMPTED TO TACKLE PIGS and slit the throats of chickens, inside the Montgomery home General William Tecumseh Sherman and members of his cavalry ran roughshod with their horses. Young Dobson watched helplessly from the shadows of the stables. The Reverend Samuel Montgomery Cowan stood in front of the Widow Montgomery and pleaded with the Federal officers to spare their home as well as their holdings.

"This is not a plantation. It is a family farm run by a widow. Your men are pillaging her property like barbarians at the gate."

Sherman was unmoved. "War is, at its best, barbarism."

"Why are you terrorizing the innocent?" the Widow asked. "We are not rebels. We are not even slaveholders. We are good, simple Christians."

"This is not about slavery. This is about the integrity of the Union."

"A Union of what?" the Reverend argued. "Forced occupation? You and your marauders lack integrity and common decency."

One of Sherman's officers struck the Reverend. The Widow Montgomery screamed. As ransacking soldiers approached the barn to seize the livestock, Dobson fled towards a tree line.

"Who is that running away?" Sherman asked. "You ask for lenience and yet you lie about your slaves?"

"He is a freeman," the Widow corrected.

Some Union officers mounted up in anticipation of pursuit.

"Never mind him," Sherman commanded. "We need to cart around more confiscated contraband like Bowie needed another Mexican. Now let's torch this hovel and keep moving."

*****

And so Young Dobson avoided the Northern Army. Only to volunteer for duty in the Rebel Army by heeding a newspaper ad.

IF YOU WANT TO HAVE SOME FUN

IN THE BACK ROOM OF A DUSTY NEWSPAPER OFFICE, Forrest and a typesetter worked out the details of an advertisement that would run in the next edition of the *Memphis Appeal.*

With his eyepiece in place, the typesetter knelt and painstakingly keyed in letters.

"Okay, sir. The headline of your ad reads '200 Recruits Wanted.'"

"Yes," Forrest enthused. "'200 Recruits Wanted.' In big, bold letters, suh."

"And the rest of your ad reads how?"

"I will receive 200 able-bodied men," Forrest recited from memory. "If they will present themselves at my headquarters by the first of June with good horse and gun. I wish none but those who desire to be actively engaged. Come on boys if you want a heap of fun and…"

The typesetter labored over the letterpress, squinted into his eyepiece and furiously keyed in the letters. "Slow down, slow down," he exhaled. "Okay: *'Come on boys… if… you… want… a heap of fun and…'*"

"…And to kill some Yankees…"

"*…To… kill… some… Yankees…*"

NOT ABOUT SLAVERY

AFTER SHERMAN PILLAGED the Montgomery home, Young Dobson stealthily headed north to Memphis. As a freeman, his safety was suspect. The Montgomerys could no longer vouch for his status, so any white men he encountered could press him into a life of servitude. Worse, after overhearing Sherman declare that the war was not about slavery, Dobson knew that not even the Yankees offered him any protection. He decided that when he got to Memphis, he would enlist in the Confederacy. Once he made it into town, he surreptitiously sought sanctuary in an outhouse. After dropping his drawers there, he found a current copy of the *Memphis Appeal.* During his perusal of the paper, he saw the ad about "killing some Yankees." Dobson told me that subsequent to what happened at the Montgomery home at the hands of Federal soldiers, if he couldn't kill some Northerners himself—he was half-blind and nobody in the South was going to give a Negro a gun, after all—with his training gotten at the Montgomery's stables, at least he could shoe the horses of the men who would. So after finishing his business and pulling up his pants, he walked out into the streets of Memphis and answered Nathan Bedford Forrest's newspaper ad.

And then he got his wish at Shiloh.

THE DEVIL'S OWN DAY

IN SHILOH, TENNESSEE, the night was a muted grey and the murkiness made it difficult to visualize the aftermath of the first day of a fierce battle. The smoke of artillery and muskets wafted slowly and fought with the gloom of a steady rain. The sound of the heavy drizzle underscored the sporadic sotto voce moans of the wounded and slowly dying. A chorus of animal grunts created a disturbing, bestial rhythm. Lightning cracked, thunder boomed and the brief rod of light cast a glimpse upon the carnage and suffering.

The whistle of artillery would follow a distant, muffled boom of cannon. The whistle would get louder and changed pitch as it approached its target. A brief blast of light flashed as the artillery hit the battlefield. As dirt, turf and human limbs flew into the air, wild hogs squealed and stopped their feeding on the dead and ran away from the point of impact. As the black of night consumed and re-subsumed the dying vestiges of light, the hogs resumed squealing, grunting and fighting each other over human flesh.

Under an oak tree next to cloth tents stood two Generals of the Union's high command. Ulysses S. Grant and William Tecumseh Sherman smoked cigars and listened to rain amidst the sporadic shelling.

"Well Grant," Sherman proffered, "we've had the devil's own day, haven't we?

Grant puffed on his cigar and thought for a moment. "Yep," he answered. "Lick 'em tomorrow though."

*****

Across the battlefield, next to captured Union cloth tents that have now become a Confederate camp, Forrest entered the quarters of General Bragg, who was in council with two Generals of the CSA high command. Bragg—a stiff angular man with crow's eyes flanked by straw hair and thick, wiry muttonchops—smoked and listened to the same rain and sporadic shelling that interrupted Sherman and Grant.

"General Bragg," Forrest said. "I have been to the river and I have seen Grant receiving troops at the landing."

"Colonel Forrest," said Bragg, "On whose authority did you go forth on your little scouting mission?"

Forrest was flummoxed. "Authority?"

"Yes, authority. General Albert Sydney Johnston is dead, so it couldn't have been him. Beauregard perhaps?"

"No suh," Forrest answered. "I have been looking for Beauregard to tell him about the arrival of the Union troops, but…"

"It is not your place to tell your superiors anything," Bragg scolded. "I am your commanding officer, Colonel Forrest."

"Yes suh. But Beauregard must know that if'n we don't keep up the skeer into the night, they're gonna whip us tomorruh'."

"Colonel Forrest, if there is anything to tell Beauregard, I will tell Beauregard."

Forrest was livid. "If the enemy come on us in the morning," he seethed, "we will be whipped like hell."

Bragg dismissed Forrest with a wave of the hand.

"Suh!" a startled Forrest protested. "I did not lead my men into battle to surrender!"

*****

In point of fact, as predicted by Forrest, after the Confederates ceded whatever ground they had won during their initial surprise attack against Grant, Bragg commanded a retreat late the next morning. To facilitate this military move, under the cover of artillery fire Forrest was instructed to launch a feint—an attack that would distract the Federals long enough for the CSA to pull back unmolested into the relatively safe confines of Corinth, Mississippi.

Later that afternoon, along green, rolling hills lined with magnolia, oak and pine trees, in a clearing known as Fallen Timbers, this final battle began as ordered—except the cannons never fired. As an ineffectual Confederate artillery squad struggled to fire a shot, much less find its target, a ragtag ensemble of Southern horsemen rode in the shadow of the impatient Nathan Bedford Forrest, whose slightly chaotic cavalry charge was in full gallop. The riders wore a motley assortment of clothes and uniforms, mostly gray and sundry earth tones whose unifying feature was a distinct lack of anything blue. Saber out, Forrest stood tall out of the saddle and led the attack.

From an adjacent ridge General Sherman watched Forrest outrun his support. "He's attacking without any artillery support. That half-cocked Secessionist sonofabitch is either fearless or has bats in his belfry."

Forrest twisted his torso towards his trailing cavalry and shouted, "Put the skeer in 'em! Keep up the skeer!"

Amidst the gathering voluminous smoke from a repetitive barrage of Yankee musket volleys, confederate soldiers pulled back on the reins of their mounts or were knocked off by the impact of gunfire. Oblivious to the carnage and the cowardice of his own troops, Forrest leaned forward and vaulted over the detritus of fallen timbers that served as earthworks for the Yankee infantry.

Forrest was in hostile territory. Alone. He had no cover fire from his cannons, which had failed to fire. He had outrun his own troops. The Federal infantry was stunned at its good fortune, as it had a Confederate Colonel within close range. They began to shoot at Forrest, and the adrenaline-charged barrage of close range musket fire created even more confusion. Forrest and his horse were both hit by Minié balls, Forrest in the left hip, and the force of the explosion momentarily lifted Forrest out of the saddle.

A startled union soldier shouted as he reloaded his musket, "Kill 'im! Kill 'im!"

Another union soldier joined the chorus, firing, reloading and shouting, "Kill the goddamn rebel! Kill 'im!"

Forrest fought for control of his horse, tugged on the reins and turned the horse around. He cleared a path amidst the mass of dark blue-clad enemy soldiers with his saber, and reached down and grabbed one of the soldiers by the collar, swinging him onto the rear of the horse. The hapless Yankee soldier became a human shield, and recoiled from a friendly fusillade of Minié balls. Forrest and his quarry galloped over the fallen timbers back towards safety. Out of range from hostile fire, Forrest let go of the dying bluecoat and his stunned men watched with their jaws dropped. He then trotted on up to a ridge where his silent cannons were staged. Among the witnesses was Young Dobson, who saw that Forrest's eyes were ablaze and saliva streamed from his lips. "Goddammit!" he shouted. "Where was my artillery cover?"

Among much murmuring, no suitable answer was forthcoming, which only further enraged the horse soldier.

"War means fighting, and fighting means killing," he exclaimed. "I will never ask you to fight anywhere I would not fight myself. Now if you follow me boys, I will always lead you to glory!"

And with that, Forrest reared up on his wounded horse and joined the exodus into Mississippi.

*****

During the retreat, the young colored blacksmith asked Forrest for permission to check the rider's wounded animal's shoes. As they spoke, Forrest took notice of a patch over the adolescent's eye. There was a flash of recognition as Forrest realized where he has seen this new recruit before: in the employ of his mother-in-law and in distress at the hands of a pair of drunken ruffians. During the examination, the two men stared at each other, briefly.

In pain, the bleeding horse whined. Forrest brushed Young Dobson aside and galloped off.

The horse died, just as he delivered Bedford to the Confederate HQ at Corinth. Despite the histrionic heroics at Fallen Timbers, Forrest nearly suffered the same fate as his valiant steed.

BRILLIANT AIN'T NUTHIN'

WHENEVER OUR TOUR GUIDE was through with an anecdote, he would blow into his harp and warble. My adjutant and I would attempt to tune out the musical accompaniment and proceed to discuss the message behind Dobson's narratives, which could often be interpreted as a parable.

"'War means fighting... fighting means killing,'" Corporal Schneider repeated. "Such simple thoughts from an equally simple man."

"Simple or erudite, Schneider?" I ruminated. "The meaning is manifold. 'When an affliction befalls you, you either let it defeat you or you defeat it.' Rousseau expressed that, suggesting, in essence, the same thing Forrest said in far fewer words. Forrest spoke like he fought—concisely yet eloquently—and both his fighting technique and his diction are genius in their irreducible simplicity. Brilliant, really."

The Negro put down his harp. "Fo' such a smart sonofabitch, you don't know shit, Lieutenant. Being brilliant ain't nuthin' if you respect nuthin' or nobody," he said, and took a hit off of his whiskey before offering a pull to me. The flask was caked with tobacco juice. I waved him off and forced a smile.

"Herr Dobson, we are not here to discuss what I do or do not know. We are here to discuss what you know, specifically about Nathan Bedford Forrest. If you would like to collect your ... what was it, Schneider?"

"Moon pies."

"*Danke.* Yes, your 'moon pies,' please keep the personal attacks to a minimum and the battle details at a paramount."

"Whatever y'all say, Mister Herr Rommel."

"Yes. Now from your accounts, I gather Forrest's troops were lacking the necessary artillery to cover their cavalry's blitzing of enemy positions. What else can you tell me about the Battle of Shiloh?"

THE LION SHALL LAY DOWN BY THE LAMB

IN THE WAKE of the two-day fight at Shiloh, a crowd of escaped yet disenfranchised slaves made camp and attempted to keep warm. Their belongings were minimal, yet strewn and gathered haphazardly around the camp. They sang in a lugubrious tone.

> *"Well the bear will be gentle*
> *And the wolves will be tame*
> *And the lion shall lay down by the lamb, oh yes*
> *And I'll be changed, changed from this creature that I am, oh yes..."*

The chorus of slaves was heard faintly at the tents that served as Grant and Sherman's HQ.

"What am I going to do with these people?" Sherman wondered.

"General Sherman," Grant counseled, "You are in a unique position to show them their freedom."

"Frankly Sir, they are a hindrance to me."

"I fear their freedom is a hindrance to us all," Grant concluded.

Oblivious to their plight and their fates, the chorus of freed slaves continued singing...

> *"There'll be no sadness, no sorrow, no trouble I see,*
> *There will be peace in the valley for me."*

"You know Sherman, I don't really care for music. I know two songs: One of them is Yankee Doodle and the other one isn't. But their music and their singing..." Grant searches for the words. "It puts my heart at peace. 'There will be peace in the valley for me, some day'..."

"Sir," Sherman declared: "We have bigger issues than the Negro problem. Our bigger concern is that Rebel horseman who has shown himself to be fearless, charismatic, brilliant or insane. You read my report on Fallen Timbers. You know that a battery of field artillery is worth a thousand muskets. This lunatic attacked without any artillery support. What happens when his cannons actually fire? Notwithstanding the simple sentiment of these darkies, I'm afraid there will be no peace in Tennessee until Forrest is dead."

*****

I MUST ADMIT I WAS FILLED WITH AWE. Ignoring Dobson's censure about "not knowin' shit," I meditated on the Negro's recollection of Forrest's extraordinary feint at Fallen Timbers, where the last shots were fired that ended The Battle of Shiloh.

"You were privileged to see an extraordinary, preternatural display of intrepid valor from an officer," I said. "It has been my experience that officers never put themselves in harm's way. You must have been inspired by his display of courage and valor."

Dobson seemed to concur: "You see a rich man in a poor man's fight, riskin' his own gen'ruh welfare to help stop a hostile invasion, you cain't help but be a little moved," he said. "Not to mention, wonderin' a little bit if the man ain't a little touched. Sho' nuff." Dobson spit more of that vile fluid out of the window of the rolling Lincoln, and a bilious cocktail of tobacco juice and saliva spackled the shell of a hapless turtle that had crawled out of the swamps and was attempting to cross the road.

THE QUEEN OF EGYPT

OUTSIDE THE MILITARY HOSPITAL in Corinth, Forrest convalesced from the gunshot wounds acquired during his daring cavalry charge at Shiloh. Young Dobson hammered on a horseshoe and watched as Bedford's family arrived for a visit. In addition to encouraging the horse soldier's recovery, the family would also celebrate his promotion from Colonel to Lieutenant General.

Seconds later, Dobson stopped working temporarily when he saw a toothsome high yella' furtively slip out of Forrest's hospital room. Dobson guessed that for Bedford and Catharine, the family's appearance was, conjugally speaking, an inconvenience they would have to wait out.

He recognized her from a few years ago, she was for sale during the auction and riot in Memphis; besides catching his wandering eye, her presence reminded Dobson of when Forrest defused a potential lynching that day. Which got him to realize that whatever the circumstances, every time he had been in Forrest's company, he witnessed the man upend superior numbers during violent confrontations. After the incidents at the creek bed, the riotous auction and Forrest's fearless wizardry at the feint of Fallen Timbers, Dobson was inspired again and again by the slave trader's intrepid valor and was elated to be in his command; now, after catching a glimpse of Forrest's fetching personal valet, Dobson was more than certain that this outfit was where he belonged. Which is to say, he admired Forrest. He also admired his mistress.

*****

Hours later, after Dobson saw Mary Forrest and the others exit, he found Catharine in the camp's kitchen.

"They gone, girl," he told her.

She nodded.

"But just the same," he smiled, "maybe you shouldn't excite him none. Maybe let him rest and keep me company."

"Where I'm supposed to keep you company? Out by the stables?"

"Come look at the stars and I'll pick the straw out of your hair."

"I tell you what: You lay down in the horse shit and I'll lay down in the warmth of the indoors, next to a cavalry rider."

"Yeah?" Dobson asked. "What you gonna lay down exactly?"

"More than you'll ever know," she said, leaving him outside. Then she stopped. "Say, what happened to yo' eye?"

*****

Inside, silhouetted from the campfires' glow that filtered through the room's small windows, Catharine curtsied. Forrest smiled, bowing his head.

After an awkward moment of silence, she said, "I heard dem' others leave and… I see you still ain't touched the broth I brought you. How you expect to get well?"

Forrest nodded his head indifferently.

"Where was we, before we's interrupted," she cooed.

"You were telling me what folks was saying."

"That's right, baby. Everyone's been talkin' about yuh, how brave yuh fought at Shiloh and how much good you's doing for the cause."

Forrest smiled. "Come closer to me, Catharine."

"Closer to what?" she sassed. "That festerin' hole? I didn't come here to open any wounds—I came to see if you livin' or dyin'. Now I seen you, I got cookin' and caretakin' to tend to."

"Woman, you're harder to keep 'hold of than a pig in shit."

"'Nuff of your devious charms," she flirted, "you wicked debbil. I'll see you 'gain when you's ready to saddle up… and ride you' favorite thoroughbred."

"You know I need to mount my favorite filly."

She lingered briefly and saucily approached the hospital bed.

Dobson's hammer began clanging in the background.

*****

Catharine exited the hospital later that night and exhaled, gathering her composure. Young Dobson had ceased banging, and caught her gaze with a furrowed look of curiosity.

"Gen'ruh taking his meals in private?" Dobson asked.

"I reckon so," Catharine answered.

"You make sho' he got his nourishment?"

"I give the man what he craved."

Her quick brash answers gave him pause. He felt his anger rise.

"How you's gonna act, woman?" Dobson demanded.

"How I's gonna act? I ain't beholden to you. I don't even knows you."

"Maybe so, woman. But you beholden to something."

"Listen fool: I do whats I gots to do to get by. I don't need to 'splain myself to you."

"Who you think you is?" he challenged. "The Lady of the Lamp? Florence fuckin' Nightingale? Or is you just the Whore of Babylon? Servin' the white man like a prostitute… I know you. I seen you on the auction block back in Mem-fus, Tennessee. Don't get high and mighty with me."

"Listen to you," she sneered. "You don't know me. You shoein' the man's shoes. You ol' Uncle Tom, ain't even gots' no cabin."

*****

As Dobson and Catharine concluded their quarrel outside, artilleryman Lieutenant Andrew Gould squared his shoulders and approached the recumbent Forrest, who was now recovering from both his gunshot wound and an excitable visit with his paramour.

"Sir, I want to congratulate you on your promotion to Lieutenant General—I am sure it is in no small part due to your audacious charge at Fallen Timbers."

"Save it, son. If you hadn't been stepping on your dick when you should have been firing off cannon support, I wouldn't have this ball up my ass."

WOMEN

THE LINCOLN PASSED a highway sign that read Highway 61. The sound of the engine permeated the Lincoln's interior. In an attempt to amuse himself and perhaps break up the tedium of our travels, Ol' Dobson resumed singing and playing the harmonica.

"Lay me down woman / 'Minister my wound / Got a hole in my heart / Black as a skulkin' coon…"

Despite the crude metaphor, I found this passage moving and I recalled a Nietzscheism. "Ahhh, women," I reflected. "A learned man once remarked that they make the highs higher and the lows more frequent."

The Negro agreed with me: "Sho' nuff, Lieutenant," he said between blows on the harp. "Sho' nuff."

*****

"So this form of music that you blithely serenade us with—it is American in form, yet African in origin? Primitive, yet lyrical."

This line of inquiry and polite conversation got no response from our minstrel. So I asked him, "It is jazz?"

"Naww man, this is the blues, baby. The blues!"

"I am not familiar with the form."

"That don't surprise me much. My guess is that a man with your upbringing and pigmentation never had much of a calling for singin' the blues."

"You never had to adhere to the Treaty of Versailles."

"And you never had your woman taken away or your house invaded."

"No. Not yet, anyway."

THE ADVANCES OF HER OPPRESSOR

OL' DOBSON CONTINUED TO BELLOW: *"A woman and a dollar are about the same."* He took a breath, riffed on his harmonica and then sang, *"A dollar goes from hand to hand, a woman goes from man to man…"*

Amidst an instrumental passage, I found a moment to interject: "I must say, Mr. Dobson, that I find this saga fascinating, if not somewhat prurient."

"What?"

"This slave girl and her philosophical and existential dilemma—not to mention her romantic quandaries."

He stopped playing. "Whatcha' getting at, Herr Rommel?"

"She had the attention of her equal and her oppressor. And it appeared she chose the advances of her oppressor. Fascinating."

Rather than solicit an answer, my acute observation seemed to inspire the man to only blow harder.

*****

Schneider drove further. Dobson toyed with his harmonica. "*Umm hmmm,*" he sang. *"You gots to serve one master or you never be free/You gots to serve one master and that'd be me."*

"It has been said," I expounded, "That 'through experience man finds to his astonishment that he is not free, but subjected to necessity.'"

I was not even sure if the black man was listening to me. He just continued to sing: *"You can call yo'sef free but that ain't true / how you's gonna act after all what they's been doin' to you?/How's you gonna act, uhh huh huh/How's you gonna act?"*

Seemingly exhausted, our troubadour put down his instrument.

"Vas was the name of that rather catchy dirge?"

The Negro pointed his harp and a meaty finger at me. "How you's gonna act?"

I must admit I wasn't sure how to answer at first. I wasn't even sure if his answer was the actual song title or a rhetorical accusation about my character. Flummoxed, I hesitated momentarily, while regaining my composure. Before the concert could resume, I rhetorically replied with my own interrogative: "I don't know, Mister Dobson. How are any of us going to act? Do any of us know how we will before it becomes our time to act?"

He "reckoned" I was right. I implored him to tell me more about Forrest's conflict with his superior officer, General Braxton Bragg. Following their power struggle on the eve of Fallen Timbers, I was curious about how either one of them would act. After all, Forrest was insubordinate. He was also right.

ANY MANNER OF GREENHORN

AT HIS HQ IN NASHVILLE, Confederate General Braxton Bragg stroked his salt-and-pepper beard and read a note from Forrest.

"Besides expressing his anger and outrage at my replacing the bulk of his mounted infantry, Forrest is also asking for an artillery specialist."

Bragg's aide was sympathetic. "He is certainly persistent, suh."

"He is the fly in my ointment."

"Yes sir. But isn't Lieutenant Gould manning Forrest's field guns?"

"Yes. Andrew Gould, a fine rational fellow. We went to West Point together. Full marks—a gentleman and a scholar."

"What is it about Gould that Forrest objects to?"

"Who knows with that uncouth maniac? Maybe he is upset that Gould never got a shot off at Fallen Timbers—which wasn't his fault; Forrest neglected to wait for the cannons to get their bearings and provide cover. Perhaps Gould mentioned that the two of us went to the academy together. Maybe Forrest resents that, being damn near illiterate. After all, giving him a military textbook would be like giving a timepiece to a billy goat."

"Pearls before swine, sir?"

"Exactly, son. To that end, let's send him any manner of greenhorn," Bragg exclaimed. "I am thinking of that rambunctious fool of a boy who is forever requesting to be transferred to Forrest's brigade, what is his name?"

"Suh, John Morton, suh."

"Yes, tawdry little John Morton—a perfect fit," Bragg repeated. "Forrest and his collection of inbred misfits are unqualified for duty. We would do well to separate the wheat from the chaff with the Army of the Tennessee and send dregs like Morton to that ill-tempered, rude hooligan Forrest."

FAULTY AND MALFUNCTIONING

WHILE DRIVING, Schneider tended to grooming matters. I found it distasteful but said nothing; in all actuality, whatever hygienic offenses my adjutant may have committed paled in comparison to the Negro's constant spitting. So I ignored it.

Instead I wanted to explore Forrest's animus with his superiors, and General Bragg, in specific. I was eager to engage Herr Dobson on his thoughts about how Forrest was able to not only overcome faulty and malfunctioning artillery equipment and its operators, but also a high command that seemed peevish and perhaps envious of the respect and awe Forrest seemed to inspire in his own men.

"When put in a position of authority," I mused, in reference to Bragg, "proud soldiers often become dubious leaders with petty agendas."

"Bragg done tried every way he could to sabotage Ol' Forrest," Dobson said. "But that just crank the Wizard up. Bragg never figgered out that Forrest was always at his best when he had the least to work with."

I raised an eyebrow as if I understood. But for the love of Odin, I often found the musings of this Negro completely obscure. In the vehicle's rear-view mirror, I caught Schneider picking his teeth with a knife; he caught me watching and looked away.

WE CAN'T MAINTAIN

AS FORREST'S CAVALRY CONTINUED ITS MARCH across Tennessee and towards Alabama, the impeccably-coiffed and erect Lieutenant Andrew Willis Gould raced on horseback to catch Forrest. Gould's formal schooling at West Point never prepared him for Forrest's blistering pace both in battle and en route to the next fight. He was rattled by Forrest's velocity. To his relief, he found the General off King Philip, his mount. Forrest's steed had a hoof that needed attention and Dobson tended to the animal's tender tendril, applying the final touches to the horse's hoof.

"May I have a word with you, General Forrest?" Gould panted.

"Certainly, Lt. Gould," Forrest replied, while mounting up. "What's on your mind?"

"Suh, I just wanted to alert you to some logistical problems we've had with the cannons."

"What kind of logistical problems?"

"Some of our guns ended up in the creek."

"How in the Sam Hain... ?" Forrest pulled on King Philip's reins and slowed the animal.

"While we trying to keep pace with your cavalry," Gould explained breathlessly, "there were too many guns on the bridge at the same time and it couldn't support..."

"Gould, you need to get your head out of your ass and wipe the brown out of your eyes."

"General Forrest, you are asking my men to haul cannons twenty-five miles and sometimes thirty miles a day. You are asking the impossible of your artillery division. Moreover, Morton, our new artillery specialist, has never fired a shot in anger."

Irate, Forrest seethed: "If war were easy, we'd get the darkies to fight it for us."

Dobson heard this, but stayed silent.

Gould, however, was indignant. "Your cavalry only has to ride on horseback," he fumed. "Meanwhile we are dragging fifteen cannons behind proud animals that are on the verge of giving up the ghost."

"Don't insult my cavalry," Forrest retorted. "When the shooting starts you get to hide on a ridge behind six-tons of iron while me and the boys are mixin' it up with the blue-bellies at point blank range."

"But we can't maintain…"

"I'll tell you what you will maintain: support and cover. In this war I've taken a goddamned Minié ball up my backside and had more than one horse drop from enemy fire. I'll listen to how hard your men and horses have it when a couple of your mounts are shot out from under you and the doc is pulling smoking hot lead out of your ass. Until that time, you better goddamned well provide me and my horse soldiers with a shroud of some serious artillery."

And with that threat, Bedford Forrest dug in his heels. He saw that his envoy could not quite keep pace and he became irate.

Of the assembled, only Dobson spoke up. "Massah Forrest, you gonna haf' to slow down."

"Damn the horses, Mr. Dobson."

"It ain't the horses, suh."

"Mr. Dobson, don't tell me it is you who cannot keep pace."

"So what if it's me, Massah' Forrest? Just because I'm black, you think I don't get tired."

FIT AS A FIDDLE

AMID A GATHERING of beaten-up, ill-clothed troops—some of whom were engaged in repairing the splintered wheels of cock-eyed cannons that had obviously seen better days—Forrest stood on a soapbox and delivered a speech to rally his weary troops. His voice carried to a distant tree line, punctuating bangs and clangs of Dobson's hammer as well as choruses of huzzahs and rebel yells.

"They said I was dead at Fallen Timbers," he bellowed, "but I am fit as a fiddle and ready for battle."

The rebel soldiers huzzah-ed.

"But you lot?" Forrest continued, interrupting the revelry. "I'm not so sure. Bragg has taken my last batch of soldiers away from me and given me a bunch of boys still suckling they's momma's tit; young 'uns who have never fired a shot in anger, nor have had to sneak up on an army twice its own size."

The soldiers murmured sheepishly in response.

"There has been some grousing about the pace of our pursuit of Abel Streight's Yankees into Alabama," Forrest continued. "They have twice our numbers. Because we are few, we can be nimble. Our only advantage is that of speed. And I intend to exploit that advantage."

The soldiers responded with more "Huzzahs!" and "Hurrahs!"

Removed from the chattering mass, Gould pulled his new apprentice—the little man named Morton—close.

"We can't exploit anything with broken cannons," he said. "This pell-mell pursuit is ill-advised at best and suicidal at worst."

"Wha-what?" Morton barely heard Gould's somber warning as Dobson's hammer clanged louder, adding further discord. "You talk like a woman. Now shut up and lemme listen to the General."

"And as we continue our defense of States Rights and the Confederacy," Forrest proffered, "let me remind you that it is our duty to fight *(PING)* to preserve our happy way of life *(CLANG)* and beat back those coward Yankees from our land *(PING)*. I've got no respect for a young man who won't join the colors *(BANG)*. And all those who do have all the honor they deserve. *(PING)* We all must do our part in this war. *(CLANG)*"

Using rhetoric and forged steel respectively, Forrest and Dobson dueled, fighting for the attention of the assembled. Irate, Forrest shouted: "Judas Priest! Will somebody tell that nigger to stop that infernal hammering!"

Dobson stopped banging and clanging on the horseshoe in mid-stroke. He looked up at Forrest, hit the horseshoe once more in defiance, then threw the hammer and walked away.

"Y'all want you horsies shoed," he muttered, "or y'all wanna keep flappin' yer gums?"

*****

"Why the incessant hammering, Herr Dobson?"

"I was as pissed off as an ol' timber rattler."

"The rest of the troops seemed to be caught up in Forrest's charisma, but you were upset at him because of the way he treated his troops? Or how he enjoyed the polyamorous spoils of power?"

"Let's jus' say the debbil gots my woman."

"This slave girl really got under your skin, didn't she?"

A LOCK OF YOUR MANE

IN FULL GALLOP, Nathan Bedford Forrest and his cavalry pursued Colonel Abel Streight's Union infantry and artillery out of Mississippi and into Alabama. The murky waters of Black Creek separated the two opposing factions. As Union artillery fired from the banks at Confederate positions, dark cedar smoke burned black and caustic, and assumed the geometric shape of a taunt.

The Confederate Cavalry converged on the banks of the creek. Among the assembled were Bedford's younger brother, Jeffrey Forrest; Gaus, a short and portly mustachioed bugler; John Morton, the fresh-faced artillery apprentice; and Lieutenant Gould. Perpendicular to the soldier, the Sansoms, a family of poor white farmers with no man around, gathered at the gates of their home, relieved that the soldiers had arrived in the wake of the Yankee destruction.

"Lt. Gould," Forrest said, "Streight has four men to my one, but Bragg's order is to overtake his guns."

"Four to one are just numbers, suh," Gould quipped. "We will take Streight's guns and continue breakin' Sherman's fingers one by one."

"There's the Tennessee spirit," Forrest marveled. "Get to those Yankee cowards before they crawl all the way to Montgomery."

With Gould properly inspired, Forrest turned his attention to the Sansoms.

"Ladies, don't be alarmed," he said. "I am General Forrest. My men and myself will protect you from harm. But I need intelligence."

Excited by the presence of the notorious Confederate leader, the widow gathered her daughters and points. "They is across the creek. And they is ready—if'n yer men show your heads—to kill the last one of you."

"Yes, yes," Forrest nodded. "I see the smoke from their fires."

Oblivious to the Wizard's strategizing, a sniper's bullet zipped through the ether and hit a rebel soldier in the face, knocking him off his horse. The soldier screamed and dropped in front of the three Sansom women, who recoiled in shock. The young man crawled in agony, his life waning.

"Get this man an ambulance!" Forrest ordered. "And take cover."

"I am afraid he is need of a hearse more than an ambulance," Jeffrey answered.

As the dying soldier was tended to, Black Bob—a grimy, longhaired, bearded horse soldier—and a handful of scouts came barreling in on their horses, kicking up billowing clouds of dust.

"Suh," Black Bob reported, "after they crossed, those Damn Yankees burnt the only bridge across the crick."

Chaos continued. Skirmishers dismounted and crawled to their places. The mortally wounded man rolled on his back, still holding his face, and expires. Muskets popped. The Widow Sansom and her daughters returned to the shelter of their home. Forrest stopped Miss Emma as she crossed through the gate of her home.

"Young Miss," Forrest implored, "can you tell me where I can get across this heah' crick?"

Mortified by the corpse at her feet and unnerved by the sporadic rifle fire, Emma Sansom spluttered: "There… there… is a rickety ol' bridge two miles away."

Forrest shook his head. "That won't do."

Fearing for her daughter's safety, the Widow Sansom yelled from her porch, "Emma! Get in here!"

Following a higher calling than familial duties, Emma ignored her mother and answered Forrest. "Well, Genr'l," she said. "There is an old ford not furthuh' than a couple of hundred yards, that the cows use to cross the crick' during dry spells. The Yankees done confiscated all our horses, but if you'n saddle me up on one of your'n horse, I will take you there."

"There is no time to saddle a horse," Forrest bellowed. "Get up here behind me!"

Forrest and Emma Sansom rode alongside the embankment, with Emma's calico bouncing against the lathered back of the steed. Alarmed, the Widow Sansom ran towards Forrest and Emma in a panic.

Livid, the Widow Sansom shrieked: "Dag blast it, Emma! What do you mean riding up there? People will talk. Do you mean to be the scandal of these heah' entire Confederate states? Get off of General Forrest's horse!

Forrest attempted to assuage the Widow Sansom's fears. "After she shows me the ford where my men can catch those Yankees," he shouted from his horse, "people will talk of her as a saint. Don't be uneasy. I'll bring her back as intact as Queen Victoria."

In full gallop, the troops followed Forrest and Emma. Amid intermittent, errant gunfire, Forrest and Emma Sansom galloped across a field and into a ravine, which emptied into a creek just above the ford. Forrest dismounted and helped Emma down. The skirmishing intensified as she guided him through bushes and briers until they reached the ford.

Forrest pulled Emma behind him.

"I am glad to have you for a scout," Forrest becalmed, "but I do not intend to make breastworks of you."

A burst of gunfire strafed Forrest and Emma, with bullets passing through Emma's billowing calico skirt.

"Miss Emma, if I may beseech you for a lock of your hair." Forrest implored.

Emma unstrung a lock of her hair and cooed: "It is my honor to grace you with a piece."

Forrest unsheathed his knife and cut off the locket. Emma recoiled as if Forrest was going to force himself on her.

"Tell your mother that I have merely relieved you of a lock of your mane," he said.

"Yes suh."

"And Emma, I need to indulge your kindness one more time."

"Suh?"

"One of my bravest men has been killed. I want you to see that he is buried in some graveyard near here."

*****

Back at the Sansom house, candles flickered as Emma and the Widow Sansom watched over the dead body of the Confederate soldier. The sounds of battle rocked the house and the ladies squinted and shuddered.

"Emma, this man's cold body is making my skin crawl."

"You hush up," Emma said. "Do your duty like Genr'l Forrest tolt' you and watch over the body of this brave, dead soldier who lost his life fighting for what's right."

SWEET MOLASSES AND SOUR SQUIRREL BAIT

AT BLACK CREEK THAT NIGHT, storm clouds gathered at Forrest's HQ. Young Dobson was by his wagon, singing a ditty about a young missus in a calico skirt, whose lock of hair made a dead man squirt. Making her way to Forrest's quarters with a cup of steaming broth, Catharine walked by and looked at Dobson queerly. A tempest was brewing, unbeknownst to Forrest, who was retiring.

"Thank you, my sweet queen bee," Forrest mewled to his mistress. "You bring me such comfort and respite in such frantic times."

"Tha's all I be a bringin' you tonight," Catharine sassed.

"As my property, you'll bring me what I ask for," Forrest exclaimed.

"Askin' one thang; gettin' a whole 'nother."

"Who put the bee in your bonnet, woman?"

"This ain't 'bout no bee in my bonnet. This about the bee who be puttin' honey on your stinger when you busy. Dobson say that sweet missus in the calico skirt maybe show you more than a way across the water. You sho' you didn't take more than a lock of her hair?"

Exasperated, Forrest exclaimed: "This is war, woman. And in times like these I answer to no one. I got no time for your minxing and meowing. I've only time for your sweet molasses and your sour squirrel bait."

The next morning, as squalls of rain peppered the troops and mucked up the roads, Forrest's cavalry continued its march in quest of Abel Streight's forces. Young Dobson was in the convoy, jockeying a wagon with Catharine as a passenger. Forrest pulled alongside his blacksmith and mistress and chewed the fat.

"King Phillip is ridin' fine through this mud, Mr. Dobson."

"Yes suh. He prancin' mighty high on this fair day. Wonder how long he can keep it up."

"What do you mean by that, suh?" Forrest wondered.

"You beat your men and your horses like they's mules," Dobson declared. "Some of them boys even asleep on they horses, not sure they' horses awake neither."

"Yes suh'," Forrest concurred. "I demand and expect more out of my men and their beasts than Abel Streight gets out of his mules. By hounding and harassing those candy-assed Yanks, we will take their freedom and we will take their guns."

"Yes suh," Dobson returned. "I'm just sayin' that sometimes death is nature's way of tellin' a man to slow down."

Forrest contemplated the paradox of Dobson's logic.

"And slowing down will be the death of Abel Streight. Thankfully that young Miss Sansom showed us passage across…"

The mere mention of the Sansom minx sent Catharine into a tizzy. "You gots to keep you's cotton pickin' hands off of some little girl's hair," she harped.

"Shut your mouth when it comes to a man's affairs, Catharine," Forrest bristled. "That means you too, Dobson."

"Me? What the…"

"Yes you, suh," Forrest said. "Keep what you see and what you think you see to yourself. Your audience hears you singing your half-backed songs and thinks she knows my affairs."

"You mean her?" Dobson wondered. "I ain't singin' to her. Whore ain't nuthin' to me but cargo."

Catharine rose off her seat, slugged Dobson in the eye and attempted to knock Forrest from his horse. Forrest blocked her fist and raised his hand to strike her. Before he could effect the blow he was interrupted by Jeffrey Forrest, who came rushing up on horseback.

"Nathan, the scouts report that Streight is headed towards Gadsen and is tearing up the railroads," he exhaled.

"That little half-wit sonofabitch thinks he Nathan Bedford Forrest? Tearin' up railroads is my job," Forrest stormed.

"I reckon so."

"Well he ain't me," Forrest thundered. "He's barely a boil on the buttocks of a Tennessee boll weevil. We will stop his destruction of Confederate property. We will wear him down and make him weak. We will devil him all night."

A NOSE FOR BATTLE

"MISS SANSOM SHOWED FORREST THE WAY 'cross Black Creek," continued Dobson, smiling. "But Colonel Abel Streight hid the Billy sharpshooters in yonder thickets of Oldfield pines. Them thickets had a sweet smell, but with his nose for battle, Forrest say that it don't matter none. He could still smell the ambush."

I was struggling to understand; I was unclear if Forrest could really smell the ambush or if Dobson was using a figure of speech. "What did he say it smelled like?"

"Like a polecat fuckin' a moccasin."

DISCUSSION IS USELESS

EXPLODED FLYING ARTILLERY cleared the Yankees from the opposite banks. The ground was muck, but the skies opened. Streight's Yankees found sanctuary in a fort. A pair of Gould's cannons took aim at the fort while, seemingly oblivious to the fusillade, Forrest called an impromptu war council of his closest subordinates, including Gould, Morton, Jeffrey Forrest, and Black Bob McCulloch. Horses belly-deep in water sludged across the creek.

"Colonel Gould," Forrest commanded, "you will cease firing upon delivery of the white flag of truce. Then you will take your cannons and parade them on yonder ridge in full view of Colonel Streight."

"Gen'rul," Gould asked, "with our miniscule artillery, wouldn't we be better represented by serving canister and grape to those Union bastards?

"What miniscule artillery?" Forrest wondered. "We have fifteen cannons."

"Gen'rul Forrest, not all of our artillery is present and accounted for."

"Gould, where the deuce are my guns?"

"Only two of our cannon units could keep up with this torrid pace of yours, General. The horses have their tongues hanging out and the rest of our artillery men are either stuck in the mud or trying to catch their breath."

"My men are meant to catch their breath when the day is done," Forrest retorted. "You sir, attempt to fetch the rest of your guns and leave me Captain Morton."

Morton took this as his cue to snap-to. "Sir!"

Gould skulked in retreat to fetch the rest of his artillery.

"Morton, those guns are miniscule only to your Captain Gould," Forrest explained. "But Colonel Streight knows not of our numbers. Take our two cannons on yonder ridge and rotate them in the shadows of the moonlight. I want him to see an armada of artillery."

"Yes, suh Gen'rul," saluted Morton.

"Black Bob," Forrest said, "until that flag of truce waves, I want you and your men to shoot at everything blue and keep up the scare. If you don't see a flag of surrender, then you and your men shall Devil them all night."

"Consider it done, suh," Black Bob saluted.

"Captain," Forrest told Jeffrey, "tell Colonel Streight that I demand immediate surrender in order to stop the further and useless effusion of blood— or I will put every man to the sword."

The barrage continued. Finally, upon Forrest's signal, the firing stopped and Jeffrey Forrest and a color bearer marched toward the Yankee fortification under a white flag of truce. Likewise, Union Colonel Abel Streight and his envoy galloped out to meet the party.

"Allow me twenty minutes to consult my officers," Streight requested.

Jeffrey proffered a flask. "Sir, I am not authorized to offer more time for strategizing, but may I offer a libation, Colonel Streight?"

Streight accepted the flask. "Why, that is a noble and dignified gesture, son."

"This might be the last drink to burn your throat," Jeffrey warned. "There ain't much refreshment in Andersonville Prison."

"As an officer with a distinguished career of battle, who has now commandeered an impenetrable fortress," Streight protested, "allow me to say that the view from our garrison suggests we are a long way from Andersonville and that an attack on such a well-armed structure is folly."

"Sir," Jeffrey genuflected, "I recognize your rank and history—not your chances."

"Such insolence under the guise of chivalry," Streight replied. "If I am to take your brother's request for surrender seriously, I need time to inventory your battery."

"You'll have nothing but time in Andersonville," Jeffrey retorted.

*****

While Jeffrey and Abel Streight bantered, Forrest observed the council of truce from his position.

"That malingerin' biscuit eater!" Forrest barked, sensing that Streight was stalling in order to count the Southern troops and perhaps wait for reinforcements. As King Phillip reared up nervously, Forrest stuffed the eyeglass into its case, tugged the reins and galloped to the meeting of Jeffrey and Streight.

"Sir!" Forrest blasted, "This is a council of truce, not a sewing circle!"

"I don't see how your cannons could've kept up in the storm," Streight said. "Allow me twenty more minutes to consult with my officers."

"You don't have twenty more minutes, sir," Forrest warned.

"Our position is solid," Streight stammered. "I must…"

"Discussion is useless," Forrest roared, pointing his long, bony forefinger at Streight. "I have known of your movements from the beginning and have been prepared to meet them. I have drawn the net tight and the only sensible thing for you to do is admit defeat."

"Sensible? Hardly, sir."

"To your left is a mountain, to your right is a river, and there is large force in your front and another force in your rear that has been gaining strength every day."

Streight looked up at the moonlit ridge where the charade of rotating cannons continued.

"Gentleman to gentleman, General Forrest," he implored. "I'm asking you: How many cannons do you possess? There's fifteen I counted already."

Forrest turned towards the guns. "Gentleman to gentleman, I reckon that is nearly all that has kept up."

Streight was indignant. "I won't surrender until you tell me how many men you've got."

"Listen heah, Colonel Streight," Forrest declared. "I reckon I've got enough men and artillery to whip you out of your boots."

"Give me a number or I will not surrender!" Streight demanded.

"You have now insulted my honor and my reputation as a gentleman!" Forrest snapped. "To Hell with this tommyrot! Gaus! Sound to mount!"

Gaus exhaled a flurry of urgent notes on his bugle. Cannons boomed and a solid shot blew a hole in Streight's men's earth works. Upon impact, deconstructed bodies flew over the parapets.

"Enough!" Streight shrieked. "I surrender, you demented, demonic wretch!"

A white flag was raised and the shelling and gunfire stopped.

"Stack your arms right along there, Colonel," Forrest beamed, "and march your men away down that holler'."

Forrest's men emerged from the shadows with shit-eating grins and began collecting the arms. Pointing at the assembled, Streight took count of Forrest's paltry numbers—a force one quarter of his own—and became apoplectic.

"Is that it?" Streight squawked. "Is that your entire force? What in the name of Judas H. Priest... General, I demand you return my arms to my men and that we should fight it out properly!"

"Ah Colonel, all is fair in love and war, you know," Forrest chortled. "Besides Colonel, sometimes a bluff beats a Streight."

Slowly building laughter among Black Bob McCulloch, Gaus the Bugler, Morton, Jeffrey Forrest and Nathan Bedford Forrest reached a crescendo. Standing alone, next to his cart, Dobson chuckled. Gould pulled up on horseback. Mutely brooding, he failed to see what was so funny.

NO DAMNED MAN

FORREST USED A MASONIC BUILDING as his field headquarters. All the windows were open, letting in a drenching heat. A discordant colonial jig played in the background. Irritated to be distracted from his work, Forrest paced. Sweat collected on his brow and mustache.

The door opened. "Sir. A Lieutenant Andrew Wills Gould to see you, sir," Jeffrey declared.

"I've been expecting him."

Entering energetically, Gould moved straight up to Forrest and stood three arms-lengths away with his hands nervously stuck into the pockets of a linen duster he wore over his uniform.

"I would like to express my gratitude in your seeing me like this," Gould said. "I realize that you are occupied, as we all are, with the detail of battle."

Forrest bowed his head slightly in recognition.

"And to that end," Gould continued, "I would like to reproach you for your conduct toward myself in the altercation against Colonel Streight. My subsequent transfer dishonored me greatly, undeservedly so, I feel, and…

"Yes, the fault is mine," Forrest acknowledged. "I foolishly trusted you with my cannons, not realizing you would ruin a brand new anvil."

"I demand an explanation for…" Gould shouted.

"So hold your tongue you insignificant, ineffectual pissant," Forrest barked. "I don't have time for you and your bellyachin'. If you are a man, go back to the field and find your lost guns. I haven't kept you from that, have I?

Forrest waved his arm in dismissal, turned his back and walked to his desk. Gould stammered out of rage and pulled a pistol out of his right pocket, walked up to Forrest, placed the pistol up against his left side and fired.   Forrest wheeled around and grunted, "Damn coward! This is why I had you transferred, you can't even kill a man that's standing next to you."

Forrest methodically grabbed Gould's pistol hand and pulled it away from his side, while with his teeth he opened the penknife in his right hand and, still holding Gould by the pistol arm, stabbed him in the abdomen. Gould dropped the gun. His face was white as he jerked away from Forrest.

Jeffrey Forrest stormed in, having heard the shot. As Gould ran out clutching his stomach and dripping blood, they collided. Gould hobbled off. Forrest wiped the blood from his knife onto his pants and collected himself.

"Call the doctor!" Jeffrey bellowed. "The General's shot!"

"It's nothing but a damned little pistol ball!" Forrest yelled.

Forrest pulled himself behind his desk, palmed two pistols himself and ran out the door, while Jeffrey Forrest sprang from his path.

A trail of blood marked Gould's route across the street to the tailor's shop where he fell onto a bench. Forrest strode into the street, hair wild, a growing stain of blood soaked through the jacket on his left side and dripping out of his pant leg. He cocked two pistols and yelled, "Where is that damned coward?"

Forrest looked straight through a gathering of astonished bystanders to an opened storefront door and an incriminating trail of blood. He passed through the store following the fresh blood. At the back porch was a young slave boy who had been practicing the fiddle. He looked at the crazed Forrest, who ignored him. Forrest quickly tracked the trail of blood with his eyes until he saw Gould about twenty yards away, running through tall grass. There was machinery and debris in the field where a small battalion of troops took gun practice. Carefully taking a bead on Gould, Forrest fired his pistol. The bullet missed and twanged off a piece of metal in the field. The bullet ricocheted and tagged a soldier in the thigh who yelped and grabbed his leg. Gould fell flat on the ground in the high grass and disappeared. Sundry bystanders and Jeffrey Forrest collected behind Forrest and followed him out to where Gould lay, shivering from loss of blood and panting with adrenaline.

Forrest raised his pistol execution style as a hand was placed on his shoulder.

"Nathan, this man is dying," Jeffrey reasoned. "Let us get you to a doctor."

Livid, Forrest ignored Jeffrey's attempt at reason. "No damned man kills me and lives!" he seethed.

Forrest lowered the pistol, cocked the hammer and, for a tender moment, looked at Gould, who was nearly unconscious.

"No suh—if some damned man killed you and lived, that would mean somehow you had a regard for at least one human life: Yours."

His eyes rolled backwards, he never heard the shot.

PISSANT OR EGOMANIAC

"IF YOU CAIN'T CARRY YO' WEIGHT
Don't complain about the freight /
If'n you burden be too great /
Don't you fret about the freight…"

"Although his death was an unfortunate eventuality, Lieutenant Gould was a distraction and, in the utilitarian sense, was rightfully terminated," I said to the Negro. "Forrest had bigger battles to fight, without having to expend energy on that… how do you say? What is the American word?"

Dobson stopped playing and took a swig from his flask. "Pissant, Lieutenant. Forrest say he was a pissant. Piss-ant."

The idiom perplexed me and inspired a smile.

"Yes, pissant. Although it is always a dilemma to merely follow orders—no matter how unrealistic—or to confront one's superiors about their untenable politics or strategy. Gould's fatal flaw was in letting his ego dictate his actions."

"Yeah, Herr Mister Rommel. That kinda' shit would never happen to you."

"That strikes me as a rather sardonic statement. Tell me, Herr Dobson: You think I'm a pissant? Or an egomaniac?"

"I think you be a horse soldier," he answered, "just like the man whose ghost you be tryin' to find. And that man wrassled with authority just like the man he kilt." Dobson spat, imbibed another swig and grinned. "Man disagreed with Forrest, got in his shit and Forrest kilt him. I leave it to y'all to figure out if this be for some so-called greater good—but after Gould died, there was nobody left in the regimen' to tell Gen'ruh Forrest he was reckless and out of control." He offered me the flask.

I hesitated before I demurred. "*Nein danke.*"

TEN THOUSAND LIVES

UNION GENERAL WILLIAM TECUMSEH SHERMAN stood outside his makeshift HQ in Jackson, Mississippi and showed his troops a note from Ulysses S. Grant.

"Vicksburg is ours," Sherman said to his soldiers, waving the dispatch as a prop. "The time is now for a design long contemplated."

A roar of bloodlust greeted the proclamation.

"We will march on Meridian," Sherman proffered, "and ultimately into Atlanta to destroy the railroad and make it impossible for the enemy to maintain any considerable force in the Trans-Mississippi. But if we are to be successful on our march, we must destroy General Forrest."

The assembled troops shouted, murmured and mumbled in general agreement and affirmation.

"Forrest is the very devil," Sherman thundered. "If we must sacrifice 10,000 lives and bankrupt the Federal Treasury to terminate him, it will be worth it."

AN OLD INJUN' WORD

IN GEORGIA, between the murk and the mud of Chickamauga Creek and the towering, wooded omniscience of Lookout Mountain, dense cedar thickets were cut to ribbons by a relentless volley of shot and shell. The smoke was a cloud of confusion that smeared all but the most abstract bursts of color: the silver glint of a steel bayonet, a blurring of blue and gray uniforms mired in a river of blood and sludge at the feet of the soldiers.

Forrest's cavalry marched hundreds of Union prisoners up mountain passages, away from the fog and haze of Chickamauga and Chattanooga.

*****

"For four days at Chickamauga Creek," Dobson recalled, "Forrest and his boys wuz busy tusslin' to git control of the bridges and such, driving back Union attacks, and hacking at the enemy's flank. We broke through the Federal lines and wuz able to push them blue-bellied Billy Yanks back into Chattanooga."

"And General Braxton Bragg?" I wondered. "He was instrumental in breaking into enemy territory?"

"Bragg? Ain't no amount of schooling would teach that boy how to win," Dobson explained. "Despite Bedford's fightin', Bragg was able to wrassle defeat out of the jaws of victory. Chattanooga was ours for the takin'. But on account of Bragg's chickenshit ways, the whole thang stalled at Chickamauga."

"Chickamauga... such a peculiar name for a battle site," I marveled. "Do you know the word's etymology?"

Dobson was puzzled.

"Origins... the word's origins."

"They say it's an old Injun' word," Ol' Dobson remembered. "But there be some controversy about what it mean. Some say it be the Injun' word for 'mud'; others say it be the Injun' word for 'more mud.'"

HARDTACK AND BULLETS

AS CAMPFIRES BURNED and mud-caked men huddled around for warmth, Forrest addressed his corps: Jeffrey, Black Bob, Morton and Gaus The Bugler. Young Dobson sat with his cart.

"Boys, yonder lies the spoils!" Forrest exhorted.

"Hardtack and bullets!" Gaus frothed.

With flying mud in his wake, a cavalry messenger in full gallop approached Forrest, who was surveying Chattanooga through binoculars.

"A note from Gen'ruh Bragg concerning your request for reinforcements, Gen'ruh," the messenger gushed. "He says we are to stop the attack and bivouac at the Chickamauga creek."

Forrest perused the note bemusedly. "Yes, that is not all."

"What else, Nathan?" inquired Jeffrey.

"He is ordering me to leave my cavalry here and to return home and start another regiment."

"That is preposterous," Jeffrey said.

Forrest was incredulous: "The man is as useless as teats on a boar... I have written to him. I have sent to him. I have given him information on the condition of the Federal army. He breaks up my command again, instead of allowing me to attack Chattanooga. I ask you Jeffrey: What does he fight battles for?"

Forrest and Jeffrey galloped to Bragg's HQ. Forrest looked calm while Jeffrey seemed a little overwhelmed, holding his hat on his head as he rushed to keep up with Forrest's long purposeful stride.

Forrest breathed in deeply. "It's a beautiful day to be without men or equipment in the middle of a war."

"You have men, Nathan. They're just under another man's command right now."

"I could have won this war months ago if I wasn't hounded by that dog Bragg. You'd think he was working for the damned enemy. That he sees it fit to separate a commander and... you shall see that this will be the last time we exchange words if I have any say in it."

THE PART OF A DAMNED SCOUNDREL

BRAGG WAS HEADQUARTERED in a small, dimly-lit one-story wooden building at Missionary Ridge outside of Chickamauga. Jeffrey and Forrest trotted up, dismounted and handed their reins to a saluting orderly. Without returning the acknowledgment, Forrest strode by the sentry. Jeffrey looked warily toward the door, pulling off his hat as he ducked in the door.

Inside the office, two aide de camps stopped attending to papers and looked up at Forrest as he stamped his boot, loosening the mud. Forrest's frame blocked much of the light coming from the doorway. Immaculate in white gloves, General Braxton Bragg stood behind his large desk while Forrest approached with his arms crossed.

"And to what do I owe this honor?" asked Bragg.

"I am not here to pass civilities or compliments with you," Forrest shouted. "I am here on rather pointed business."

"Not as pointed as your business with Lieutenant Gould, I assume."

"We shall see, suh'."

Bragg sat down, his face drawn with both surprise and extreme agitation. "General Forrest, may I remind you that in spite of your recent promotion by the War Department, you are still addressing an officer of superior rank."

"Don't feed me that West Point officer bullshit," Forrest retorted. "Your high-and-mighty alma mater may have taught you how to read a textbook, but apparently you missed the chapter on common sense."

"Sir!"

"Yes, suh'! All that book learnin' has only taught you how to run an army into the ground. Every time the fighting gets a little thick, you run like a dysentery dog."

"General Forrest! Enough of your insolence! I must remind you of whom you are addressing!"

"Shut up and listen, you yellow-bellied cur!" Forrest bellowed. "You commenced your cowardly and contemptible persecution of me soon after the battle of Shiloh, and you have kept it up ever since. You robbed me of my command in Kentucky, men that I armed and equipped with the spoils taken from the enemies of our country. Because I would not fawn upon you as others did, you drove me into West Tennessee with a second brigade I had organized, with improper arms and without sufficient ammunition, although I had made repeated applications for the same. You did it to ruin me and my career."

"This is pure balderdash, General Forrest," Bragg declared. "Because we are grossly outnumbered, our defense of this land often requires a nimble shuffling of manpower and munitions."

"Well, suh," Forrest said. "You have just described your weakness as a commanding officer: you think only in terms of defense when you should be attacking offensively."

"Attack with our inferior numbers and munitions?" Bragg coughed. "You are mad as a hatter and…"

"And you are a petty crab and a hindrance to victory," Forrest interrupted, wagging an index finger at Bragg. "When, in spite of all of this, I returned with my command well equipped by captures, you began again your work of spite and persecution, and have kept it up. And now with my present brigade, organized and equipped without thanks to you or the government, a brigade which has won a reputation for successful fighting second to none in the army, and we stand at the ready, poised to take Chattanooga and capture Rosecrans and you are standing in our way."

Browbeaten, Bragg grabbed the armrests of his large, overstuffed chair. All the while Jeffrey stood silently, hat in hand.

"I have stood your meanness as long as I intend to," Forrest continued. "You have played the part of a damned scoundrel, and you are a coward. If you were any part of a man I would slap your jaws and force you to resent it."

"You, sir, are ignorant and know nothing of politics," Bragg admonished. "You have but one virtue… No, virtue is the wrong word for the likes of you. You have one talent, which is to say you are nothing but a good raider. Other than that, you are nothing to me but a subordinate—and now an insubordinate."

"Listen, you foppish dandy," Forrest fired. "This tactical retreat is madness. We have Old Rosey and his damn Yankees right where we want him, right down there in Chattanooga. If you do not intend to fight, then perhaps it is best to send me to another command where I can make a difference. I will be in my coffin before I will fight again under your command."

"Yes, prepare to transfer your command," Bragg advised. "I am sending you and your band of crackers back to Mississippi. And I say to you 'good riddance.'"

"And I say to you that if you ever again try to interfere with me or cross my path, it will be at the peril of your life."

Without letting his message sink in, Forrest left abruptly, nearly knocking over Jeffrey, who then followed him out after a slight nod to the astonished Bragg.

The men mounted their horses and rode back towards their camp. Forrest was silent.

"After that tirade," Jeffrey said, "you may as well hang up your saddle because when Jefferson Davis hears about this in Richmond, your command is history."

"No," Forrest said. "Bragg'll never say a word about it to Richmond—he'll be the last man to mention it. And mark my words, he'll take no action in the matter. I fully expect to read of the Federals keeping Chattanooga. We should wrap up Chattanooga, and tie it with a bow."

*****

I WAS APOPLECTIC: "This is how wars are often lost, with such foolish insubordination. Forrest may have been a strong fighter, but he would never be a true warrior without honoring the contract he had made with his superiors—a contract which held together the cause he fought for."

Ol' Dobson wasn't buying it. "That doesn't mean shit," he said. "The only contract a man has to honor is the deal he makes in his heart. You can call that insubordination if you wanna."

The Negro took his flask and pulled a long one.

TICKLES THE HEAVENS

WITH COLORS FLYING GRANDLY, a massive, awe-inspiring phalanx of Union cavalry, infantry and artillery under the command of General William Tecumseh Sherman made a dusty march through the countryside. Everything was blue, black and orange. In their wake, smoke from their trail of destruction tickled the heavens and sullied the clouds. It was Jackson, Mississippi and it was on fire.

*****

"IT WARN'T ENOUGH that Forrest had to fight the cowardice and incompetence of his immediate superiors," is how Dobson put it. "From time to time he also had to fight the real enemy: he had to stay one step ahead of that firebug Sherman."

"Ah, General Sherman," I beamed. "I read his book."

"I'm supposing he mentioned something 'bout Forrest, Herr Lieutenant?"

"He did, indeed. Sherman's distaste and reluctant admiration for Forrest's unconventional methods has truly been a principle catalyst for my journey here," I said.

"Round these parts you just mention the name Sherman and folks kinda' wanna' clear they throats." Dobson spat.

"*Warum ist das?*"

"He burnt they' shit down, boy! They burnt the widow's shit down!" Dobson shouted, causing Schneider to take his eyes off the highway momentarily and turn his head. "Not everybody heah' a plantation owner wif' slaves. Most folks heah' didn't even have a dog in the fight."

"Rich man's war, poor man's fight."

"Sho' 'nuff, Lieutenant."

The Lincoln motored past a sign that read: "OKOLONA CITY LIMIT POPULATION 835." We were getting closer to Forrest's fabled crossroads.

THE SOONER IT WILL BE OVER

IN THE CENTER of Meridian, Mississippi, amidst smoldering devastation, General Sherman and Brigadier General Samuel Sturgis trotted on horses, surveying the carnage and admiring the thoroughness of their work. A mounted messenger delivered news of Forrest's return to Mississippi and his subsequent vandalizing of Union trains and supply lines to General Sherman.

"General, news of the guerilla raids between here and Memphis," the messenger reported, presenting the cache to Sherman.

Sherman handed it to Sturgis. "Tell me what it says, Sam."

"Bragg sent Forrest away from Chattanooga," Sturgis said, "and Forrest and his new greenhorn cavalry are tearing up the railroads across Kentucky and Tennessee."

Sherman tugged on the reins. "We can destroy the Confederate infrastructure with as much panache and enthusiasm as Forrest brings to his work."

"Permission to speak frankly, sir," Sturgis implored. "I will follow your command and destroy the Secesh railroads, their homes and their plantations. And I will get Forrest. But with all due respect, General, if we resort to more ruthlessness against the general population does that not make us as uncivilized as the very Devil and his band of guerillas?"

"I cannot second-guess my command because of cries of barbarism," Sherman scowled. "The plight of the common man is not my concern, Sam. War is cruelty. There is no use trying to reform it. The crueler it is, the sooner it will be over."

"Yes, but when it is done will we have destroyed the means of any man—including the emancipated slaves—to grow his crops and keep a roof over his head?"

"Listen, man," snorted Sherman. "We are not here to make friends with the mint julep society. We are not here to help the niggers. We are here to end this cruel war."

The sky was red with fields of burning corn and cotton. Union soldiers and contraband-freed blacks set the torch to mansion houses, stables, and cotton fields, leaving only embers in their wake.

YOU MAY BURY MY BODY

TO THE CHAGRIN of my adjutant, from the back seat of our automobile Dobson continued his singing and playing.

> *"You may bury my body*
> *down by the highway side*
> *Baby, I don't care where you bury my body*
> *When I's dead and gone*
> *You may bury my body, oohh*
> *Down by the highway side*
> *So my old evil spirit*
> *Can catch a Greyhound and ride."*

TIME ISN'T PARTICULAR

IN THE HILL COUNTRY of Mississippi, a battle flared sporadically amongst fields of corn, soybeans and cotton. To the Almighty toying with his abacus, it was immediately apparent that the Union Troops under Sturgis had far superior numbers to Forrest's troops. During a smattering of random gunfire from sharpshooters, Forrest's cavalry prepared to charge, but some of the men hesitated. Forrest stood tall in the saddle, alternately looking forward and over his shoulder.

"C'mon boys!" shouted Forrest. "The safest place is over yonder! Come on! Follow along here, and pretty soon there will be a fight over yonder, and you can get you some Union guns."

His troops began to stir, slowly generating a forward momentum, but their velocity did not meet Forrest's expectations. The Wizard pulled up his horse and addressed his advancing cavalry. "Fear not, my boys, because it is those Yankees who are badly skeered."

In a wooded area thick with pine trees, while crossing a rickety bridge about thirty yards long, Forrest and his minions encountered a firefight. As they reached the other side of the river, a panic-stricken Confederate soldier fled the battle, and tossed away any material—hat, gun, knapsack—that could weigh him down and hinder his flight.

Forrest jumped from his horse, grabbed the soldier and began beating him with a tree branch.

"What are you doing, son?" Forrest demanded.

"The skeer...." the soldier cried. "The skeer..."

Forrest swatted and pummeled the cowering soldier. "Why you cowardly skunk! Don't you know it is a privilege to die in the defense of your entire way of life?"

The soldier offered token resistance and endured a severe beating. Forrest turned the soldier around and pointed him towards the source of the battle.

"Now, Goddamn you," he barked, "go back there and fight; you might as well be killed there as here, and if you ever run away again you'll get more than a beatin' with a switch."

That night Dobson shod Forrest's horse as Forrest exited his tent.

"How is King Phillip?" Forrest inquired.

"Well, he too proud to show it," Dobson reckoned, "but he is wore out and tore up, as usual, from all that keepin' up the skeer."

"Well that may be, but I'm depending upon you to prep King Phillip thoroughly, Mr. Dobson. Come tomorrow on the field of battle, the Federals gonna know the skeer'. When they hear Gaus blow his bugle, they will know their time has come."

"Yes sir," Dobson nodded, "you just 'member that Time ain't real particular about who it come for."

THEN WE WILL CHARGE THEM

A FIREFIGHT RAGED. Cannons exploded and casualties were thrown from their horses. Among the hardest hit were Tennesseans under the command of Colonel Clark Barteau. Forrest galloped upon the skirmish with his hat upraised, in acknowledgement of cheers from his soldiers.

Pulling the reins, Forrest calmed his horse. "Where is the enemy's whole position?"

Flinching from pinging bullets, Barteau answered: "You see it, General and they are preparing to charge."

"Then we will charge them. Jeffrey! Black Bob! Take your divisions to their flank. You, Jeffrey, to the west and Black Bob to the east. Each of you find their thinnest points and charge, asking no quarter."

Saber raised and pointing, Forrest shouted and charged. The Union line crackled with fire. Following their commander's orders, the brigades of Jeffrey Forrest and Black Bob McCulloch got caught in the volley. McCulloch was wounded in the hand, but Jeffrey Forrest was struck and felled by a ball through the neck. Shaken and stunned, the two brigades ceased their charge upon the fall of their leaders.

Forrest rode onto the scene and dismounted to cradle his fallen brother.

"Jeffrey… Jeffrey… Jeffrey…," Forrest wept.

Jeffrey gurgled blood and died. Forrest laid his brother down and covered his face, and continued kneeling while surveying the field.

Forrest summoned his bugler, "Gaus! Sound the charge!"

Gaus raised an instrument dinged and dented with bullet holes and complied with the order.

Forrest mounted up and pointed his steed towards the Federal line that had just shot his brother. A line of five hundred soldiers dispersed, and then re formed, nervously.

Oblivious to having left many of his stunned cavalry in his wake, Forrest pierced the Federal line and began attacking the assembled Yankees, dropping the reins of his frightened horse. With eyes glazed with anger, Forrest unsheathed his saber, drew his six-shooter and systematically attacked any man who might be his brother's killer, single-handedly slaying three unlucky Yankees with his sword and his pistol.

COGITO ERGO SUM

IN THE CAR, I WAS AGLOW.

"Death would immobilize a lesser man," I reasoned. "Even as his brother succumbed he was a man of action."

Old Dobson sipped at his flask. "If action defines the man, then that man'd be Bedford, who thought and then he wuz'."

"Yes, yes, of course," I said. "Like the Cartesian axiom, *Cogito ergo sum.*"

"'Cept'n sometimes Forrest just dispensed with the thinkin' part."

The Negro took another snootful, and then offered me his flask. Once again, I declined. Herr Dobson then told me the last details of Okolona, before giving me a first person account of the most contentious and controversial of Forrest's triumphs, the Battle of Fort Pillow. All the while on a neglected two-lane highway, we crept closer to the crossroads, west of Tupelo, Mississippi.

FIX BAYONETS

FORREST WAS JOINED by an escort of sixty horse soldiers who were in furious hand-to-hand combat with the line of five hundred Federal soldiers.

McCulloch's brigade came in full sweep, but halted when they saw the makings of a trap before them.

McCulloch waved a bandaged, bleeding hand. "My God, men, will you see them kill your general? I will go to his rescue if not a man follows me!"

McCulloch's Brigade caught up with Forrest and the pursuit continued. Amongst McCulloch's men was Young Dobson, the brigade's blacksmith. As they penetrated a second Federal line, Forrest's horse was hit and the saddle shattered.

"Gen'ruh, I thinks you should get that ass out of the road," Dobson warned amidst the pandemonium, "it ain't right to expose you own self unnecessarily."

"Dobson, if you are alarmed," Forrest rejoined, "you may get out of the way. I am as safe here as there."

Fighting was sporadic, yet fierce. Artillery shells pounded Forrest's position and knocked his horse down, killing the stallion.

Dobson dismounted. "Gen'ruh, please take my horse."

Forrest waved Dobson off and ordered a Private in his escort to relinquish his stepper. "Go to the rear, son."

As Forrest climbed upon the animal, five Yankee bullets shattered the saddle, killing the poor beast. Through the continued skirmishing, Forrest picked up a musket, gathered a few men and charged on foot through the back yard of a farmhouse. There, Dobson caught Forrest and presented him with King Phillip, his favorite and venerable (if not sluggish) steed, which was also shot—the third horse to catch enemy fire that afternoon. The beast stumbled, but remained erect.

Forrest and his men drew a line of battle. Throwing down their rifles and drawing their six-shooter pistols, they repulsed a ferocious cavalry charge.

"Fix bayonets!" Forrest commanded. "Forward men! And mix with 'em!"

The combat became hand-to-hand. Black Bob McCulloch was among those out of ammunition and had only an empty carbine. A Federal officer took aim upon McCulloch as Forrest rode up on a wounded King Philip and with a sweep of his saber severed the Northern officer's head from his shoulders. The officer toppled as Black Bob grabbed his revolver, mounted up on a rider-less horse and charged into battle.

After a fifth Federal line broke and was vacated, soldiers scattered pell-mell.

Forrest heard moans of agony issuing from a hut that served as a makeshift hospital.

Inside, a Federal soldier in the midst of having his leg amputated had a saw stuck in his bone marrow, as left by a fleeing surgeon. Forrest applied chloroform to his handkerchief and tranquilized the victim, before finishing the amputation.

"I cannot stand to see a job half-finished," Forrest muttered.

The wounded soldier raised up as if undead, and then passed out. His vengeance slaked, Forrest beat a hasty retreat back into his own camp.

Forrest and his cavalry regrouped and were in the process of tending to the after effects of battle. Wounds were cleaned, meals cooked and horses shod. In the background, Catharine tended to a cauldron.

In the distance, towards a tree line, dead horses burned in a funeral pyre.

TO GET BY

DESPITE HIS EXHAUSTION from battle, Forrest climbed between the sheets with Catharine, engaging in coitus and bittersweet moments. She whispered in his ear and made him laugh, temporarily taking his mind off the loss of his brother.

By the campfire, as Young Dobson banged away on the shoes of King Philip, he heard the sounds of erotic playfulness coming from inside Forrest's tent, and as the passion inside the tent reached a muted crescendo, the hammering on the horse's hooves clanged louder and faster.

Catharine exited Forrest's tent and encountered Young Dobson's steely glare. "After all that shit he put you through on the auction block you sneak 'round dustin' his broom...?"

"That man lost his brother today..." she reasoned.

"You don't need to 'splain yourself to me, woman," Dobson interrupted. "Like you say: We all gots to do what we gots to do to get by."

"Sometimes," Catharine teased. "Sometimes you just got the want to's."

ONLY ONE WAY TO ANSWER A MAN

TECUMSEH SHERMAN read the accounts of Okolona to Sturgis from the newspaper, the *Cincinnati Commercial.*

"And I quote, 'Forrest, with less than four thousand men, has moved right through the Sixteenth army corps, has passed within nine miles of Memphis, carried off one hundred wagons, two hundred beef cattle, three thousand conscripts and innumerable stores, tore up railroad track, cut telegraph wire, burned and sacked towns, run over pickets with a single derringer pistol, and all, too, in the face of ten thousand men.'"

"General," Sturgis said, lowering the newspaper, "with our superior abilities and our superior numbers, we shall blunt and upend the attacks of the so-called 'Wizard of the Saddle.'"

"There is only one way to answer a man like this," Sherman concurred, "and that is to break him utterly. We will crush him mechanically."

BLACK SNAKE ON THE BANKS

FORREST'S TROOPS BIVOUACKED on the tranquil banks of the Tennessee River. The air was redolent with burning twigs, smoldering bacon and chicory substituting for actual coffee. The crackling of the fires melded with the echoes of un-tuned banjos and men wagering what was left of their wages over poker hands. Forrest slept. With no time to rest, Catharine used this moment to take some washing to the banks of the river. Stealthily, Dobson followed her.

"You still got the want-to's, woman?"

"I ain't studyin' no muthafuckin' blacksmith."

"You best be studyin' sump'n, woman. Be careful you don't get bit by this ol' black snake."

"I bet that ol' black snake don't bite none. Might forgot how, cuz it ain't been fed in a coon's age. Ain't that right, daddy?"

Dobson said nothing. His answer could be heard in the sounds of the river, as the water lapped on the silt of the shores, receded slightly and repeated itself.

FORMING

AFTER HERR DOSBON CONCLUDED HIS SALTY, RIBALD ANECDOTE about unrequited lust on the banks of the Tennessee River, he requested that Schneider stop our vehicle, as his (Dobson's) "ol' black snake" was a "spitting trouser adder," and sometimes this viper would unleash its venom indiscriminately.

In point of fact, he said, this serpent needed immediate relief. I told the rather befuddled Schneider that I thought this meant that our passenger needed to urinate, and to pull over onto highway's edge.

Dobson carefully manipulated his rather angular, antediluvian body out of the sedan and began splattering the sweltering Mississippi asphalt with the waste from his bladder, with the resulting transfer of heat and atomization of liquid creating a foul, bilious steam.

Just off the highway, there were entire forests and swamps that would serve as a more natural and reasonable receptacle for the black man's urine, but instead he insisted on pissing on the pavement with the unstated rationale being that the sizzling, wafting vapors would serve as an unpleasant reminder of the messy and odious American Negro problem—or at least, this was my extrapolation. Indeed, even after slavery was outlawed, theirs was a situation more vexing and perplexing, and a social dilemma never properly handled by the United States of America. Here, the freed black denizens and their descendants were relegated to second-class citizen status, which is to say in a sort of limbo—not actual bondage, but not entirely free either. And they were not happy.

Yes, the urination was a subtle, symbolic statement. Old Dobson knew what he was doing. He always had, going back to his employment with the Montgomerys and even more so during his tenure under Forrest. And in this instance, he let me know he could be as vexatious as he wanted to, and I would have to be as pleasant as possible in return. The reason being, of course, was that Old Dobson was perhaps the only man still alive that contained the knowledge necessary to inform the battle strategies and theories that were forming in my mind, as I prepared for the inevitable future hostilities, while co-opting the nimble, ferocious cavalry style employed by Bedford Forrest in his vicious attacks against unsuspecting and under-prepared Yankee forces. So I sat there, thinking of how my future and Dobson's past were inextricably intertwined and suffered the stench of urine.

*****

And there we were, en route to Brice's Crossroads. Metaphorically speaking, I was at a crossroads in my career. But Herr Dobson had already passed through them, seventy years ago. He was conflicted, and as we got closer to the place of the defining moments of his own history, he didn't seem to be particularly enthralled with the idea of revisiting them.

But before we would arrive at our destination, he had time to tell me about the notorious Battle of Fort Pillow, the engagement that preceded Brice's Crossroads, and an event that struck many as an exercise in barbarism, if not actual genocide.

Fort Pillow's point of contention concerned the alleged attempted surrender of four hundred Negro Union soldiers, who gave up their guns and still fell at the feet of Forrest's conquering marauders. Did Forrest himself order their execution?

Whatever their fate and whatever Forrest's role—and even though I am a man who always followed a certain military code—the situation surrounding their demise was not really my concern. Even so, it was enough to really agitate many people who remember the details of that fight, including George Dobson, who relieved his bladder on that very highway that led to those crossroads.

FIGHTIN' JOE HOOKER'S GIRLS

AT FORT PILLOW, Tennessee, Federal soldiers—mostly black—went about their daily lives. The compound was protected by prominent artillery, manned by black Federal soldiers.

At the supply store, rats scampered amongst barrels of whiskey, and stores of grain, cotton and ammunition. A gathering of prostitutes loitered outside the store. Somewhat discreetly, money changed hands between a pair of white soldiers of different rank.

Inside, the store was dark and musty. It stank of inebriation, corruption and general debauchery. Like the men and the perfumed ladies, it needed a bath, if not a haircut. A slovenly quartermaster stood behind his counter, and was flanked by a white union soldier, sitting lazily on a powder keg, helping himself to sporadic ladles of whiskey.

"Hey storekeep'! How much for a woman?" a black union soldier asked the quartermaster.

The quartermaster laughed. "More than you can raise, nigger. You may be free these days, but there are some things you can't buy in these parts. The women are for the white men."

From the shadows, a loitering white union soldier interjected, "Yeah nigger: Ain't nuthin' in Mr. Lincoln's E-man-suh-pay-shun croc-luh-may-shun about the black man gettin' any white tail. There's be a whole 'nother war over that shit, right after this one is finished."

"You mean to tell me those harlots' honey pots lined with gold?" the black soldier asked. "These tramps the daughters of King Midas or sump'n?"

"These girls served under Fightin' Joe Hooker at Chancellorsville and across the commonwealth of Virginia," the quartermaster explained, "and followed Hooker and his men all the way to Vicksburg."

"Yeah, well you can keep Hooker's used-up river trash," the black union soldier spat. "I reckon a couple a ladles of that mash whiskey and I'll pet my one-eyed snake and just dream of a seafood store."

"It's two bits a ladle, nigger," the quartermaster explained. "Less'n you intend to pay with some of the Confederate money you and your porch monkeys been stealin' from helpless Confederate widows down in Mississippi. Then it's a whole lot more."

"No need to harass the white folks this week," the black soldier replied. "Mr. Lincoln and the War Department finally done paid me for services rendered in the defense of liberty and the preservation of the Union. I am a professional soldier, same as you. So gimme four dips of your rotgut, storekeep. Here's a Union greenback."

In a defiant move, the white union soldier put his boot on the lid of the whiskey barrel.

"I'd be much obliged if you's remove your shit-kickin' foot from the whiskey barrel, white man," the black union soldier warned.

Smirking, the white soldier slid his boot off of the barrel.

"Sure thing… boy."

"Boy?" The black soldier took umbrage. "You better feel again, soda cracker. Put out your hand and I'll make sure you know you ain't dealin' with no boy."

The quartermaster laughed.

The black union soldier removed the lid and proceeded to spoon whiskey down his gullet. His countenance alternated between a grimace and a smile.

"These niggers gettin' pretty full of themselves pretty sudden-like," the white soldier snorted. "It's one thing to take away the chains, it's another to give 'em our women—even if it's just Hooker's girls."

"Though it goes against my principles, I am about tempted to sell them the hookers," the quartermaster sighed.

"Have you lost your sense of decency?" the white soldier said.

"Hey fuck you, white boy," shouted the black soldier, pointing the whiskey ladle. "My money green too."

"It ain't about the color of money," the quartermaster answered. "Ever since Uncle Billy took the proper white troops for himself and left me with you homemade Yankees and free niggers, business ain't been worth shit."

"That's because Uncle Sam give us black folks half the money," concluded the black union soldier. "Half the money mean half the whiskey and half the poontang."

"I know Sherman is crazy as a Catahoula cur," said the white soldier, "but what kind of ignorance makes a man to leave all the drunk and lazy black troops to guard against Confederate attacks?"

"Lucky the other day was payday," the quartermaster said, "and most boys are drunk and happy. 'Course some of the niggers been harassing the residents of their old plantations. If that keeps up, you better brace for a dose of Nathan Bedford Forrest, who ain't gonna put up with that shit."

"I ain't studyin' no motherfuckin' Nathan Bedford Forrest." The black man said into the whiskey ladle.

The quartermaster was somber. "Yes. Well, be advised he be studyin' you."

FORT PILLOW

CONFEDERATE AMMUNITION WAGONS ARRIVED upon the perimeter of Fort Pillow. Soldiers were preparing for a siege, as Forrest did reconnaissance in the shadows of the fort, looking for a weakness. Sporadic gunfire buzzed the CSA position. Shells from a Union gunboat, the *New Era*, pounded the Confederates. A bullet whizzed and pinged King Phillip and the horse reared with pain and fright and was stricken dead. Young Dobson rushed to Forrest's aide and pulled him from the stricken mount. Without missing a beat, Forrest climbed on Dobson's horse.

"Suh," Dobson declared. "You should finish your inspection on foot."

"I am apt to be hit one way as another," Forrest rationalized, "and I can see better where I am. And from terra firma I can see we have a numerical advantage. Fetch me my writin' utensils."

Skirmishing and sporadic gunfire from sharpshooters continued, while Forrest feverishly scribbled with a quill.

"Now Dobson," Forrest demanded, "fetch Black Bob and send him forward with a flag of truce and this note."

Outside the fort, representatives from both factions of battle assembled outside the garrison. On horseback, Black Bob McCulloch and Major Booth— a Federal officer—faced each other.

Black Bob read Forrest's note to Booth, while struggling with the bigger words: "As your … gallant defense of the fort has entitled you to the treatment of brave men, I now demand an un… un… unconditional surrender of your force, assuring you at the same time that your men will be treated as prisoners of war. I have received a fresh supply of ammo… ammunition, and can easily take your position. Should my demand be refused, I cannot be res- … responsible for the fate of your command."

"Right," said the federal officer dismissively. "And a bluff beats a straight."

Forrest took a position on a bluff overlooking Fort Pillow.

Black Bob returned and reported, "He says your demand does not produce the desired effect."

Flummoxed, Forrest shouted, "This will not do! Send it back and say to Major Booth that I must have an answer in plain English, yes or no! You can tell that damn Yankee that if I am compelled to butt my men against their works, it will be bad for them."

Forrest rode out in front of his cavalry. Black soldiers inside Fort Pillow began shooting at him. Others jeered, grimaced and made lewd gestures, including dropping their pants.

Behind ravines and shanties, Confederate soldiers laid quietly, within one hundred yards of the fort. Forrest arrived on horseback among a collection of corpses and cowering soldiers, hidden in a ravine and behind trees and logs to avoid an exasperating fire from the fort and the gunboat, which continued its shelling.

"Who is in charge of these men?" Forrest asked.

"I am," a gaunt, thinly-mustachioed soldier saluted. "Lieutenant French at your service, suh."

"Lieutenant," Forrest said. "I am ordering you to advance."

"General, that is death."

"Perhaps you did not hear me above the din," Forrest seethed. "I am ordering you to advance."

French complied and started forward. "Advance on that fort, men!"

As a few hardy souls rose up to attack, the garrison's sharpshooters immediately opened fire, sprinkling the ground with Minié balls. The men stayed put. French scurried ten steps forward then dived behind a log, where bullets hacked and chipped at the bark. Awaiting further orders, he wondered if his commander has lost his marbles.

On the banks of the Mississippi River, several Union steamships attempted to dock under fire from Morton's guns.

"Take two companies and slip behind the fort," Forrest commanded Black Bob. "Fight everything between wind and water until yonder flag comes down."

Turning to an aide, Forrest said, "Go to Colonel Barteau and tell him when he hears my bugler, to go over the works even if he and every man in his command is killed, and tell him I don't want to hear of Tennessee being left behind."

Grabbing another aide, he said, "As soon as you drop into yonder ditch, your men will stoop down and serve as a ladder for those soldiers behind you."

As Gaus raised the bullet-dinged bugle and sounded the charge, an explosion of fire blasted from the fort, but was drowned out by a deafening chorus of rebel yells.

CSA sharpshooters decimated those guarding the fort, including a host of black artillerymen. Bell and McCulloch reached the center of the works concurrently, trailing their men, who were engaged in a merciless slaughter of black and white soldiers. Among the more violent perpetrators were the two ruffians who had once menaced Young Dobson, when he was under the employ of the Montgomerys as a chauffeur.

A cluster of bedraggled prostitutes escaped in a wagon. From her carriage, Catharine exchanged glances with a prostitute who was missing a tooth. Catharine's countenance was tinged with both empathy and contempt.

Concurrently, fleeing Union soldiers attempted to rendezvous with the *New Era* gunboat, which had refused to dock and was back-pedaling into the murky waters of the Mississippi River. With their rescue vessel beyond their reach, the hapless black and white Union soldiers were caught in a triangulated crossfire between Black Bob's regiment and a company of Barteau's men. Those who outran the two-pronged attack leapt into the river and struggled to say afloat. Many drowned.

Young Dobson and his wagon were parked on a bluff overlooking the reddening river. He saw black soldiers bleeding, dying and drowning in the river.

"Mercy sakes," he whispered.

BURY THE DEAD

AT DUSK THE FEDERAL FLAG CONTINUED TO FLY. It was bedlam inside the fort. Spigots opened as thirsty rebel soldiers tapped into buckets of whiskey and barrels of ale; it was a bacchanal of blood and whiskey, as the men divided their time between boozing it up and slaying fleeing black soldiers.

One wounded Negro soldier attempted to surrender to some of Forrest's men. Instead, he was shot point blank in the face and bayoneted in the heart.

As more shells from the *New Era* landed inside the fort, Forrest arrived on foot. He pointed to the tattered American flag fluttering in the wind and barked out orders.

"Cut down that blasted flag and restore the proper colors," he bellowed.

Forrest surveyed the carnage. He caught sight of the ruffians, Dobson's former tormentors. They smiled. He didn't.

"We have the rule of what was once a fort and is now Hell's half-acre," Forrest said. "Now we must bury the dead."

As Forrest speechified, Catharine abandoned her wagon and ran towards the safety of the *New Era* gunboat. Upon entry, and to her surprise, this was where "Hooker's girls" had also taken sanctuary.

GONNA CARRY SOMEBODY ELSE

IN THE LINCOLN, the tourists were stunned by Ol' Dobson's account of what was, in essence, genocide. Much to my resigned bemusement, once again our Negro tour guide pulled out his harmonica and began playing and singing.

"Painted ladies don't wanna
Climb on George's saddle
They run from the rebels
Like they's so much cattle"

KNOCKED ME TO MY KNEES

AS THE FIGHTING UNWOUND and the bodies were dragged to improvised graves, a sporadic bombardment from the enemy ship's guns muddled matters. Forrest addressed a handful of soldiers: "Turn those Yankee guns around and aim them towards the mighty Mississippi and blast the shit out of that infernal gunboat."

Finally, the shelling ceased. Forrest then gathered his officers and pointed to the high ground upon which Gaus had sounded his charge. He then placed his right hand on his left breast.

"When from my position on that hill I saw my men pouring over these breastworks," he said, "my heart burst within me. Men, if you will do as I say I will always lead you to victory. I have taken every place that the Federals have occupied in these parts except Memphis and if they don't mind I'll have that place too in less than six weeks. They killed two horses from under me today and knocked me to my knees a time or two, so I thought, by God, they were going to get me anyway."

DISAPPEARS IN DEFEAT

HERR DOBSON CONTINUED his serenade.

"I don't pick no cotton and I don't raise no corn,
If I see a mule runnin' away with this world,
I'm goin' to tell it to go 'head on."

This last piece of doggerel was more than Schneider could take. Quick as an adder, he reached into the back of our sedan and snatched Dobson's mouth organ in mid-wheeze. "What in der hell does that verse even mean?" he cried, as he whisked the instrument out of the moving car's window and into some neglected cotton fields.

"What the...?" Dobson yelled. "Why are white folks always fucking with my harmonica?"

Although I could sympathize with his being angry, I can't say I felt terribly compelled to apologize or even discipline my adjutant for his impetuous behavior. His simple discordant din was rather hard on our European ears.

During the refreshing silence, Schneider parked the motorcar. Dobson and I waited inside as my adjutant urinated.

"Don't you think that for political purposes," I suggested, "the fight at Fort Pillow has been represented as a barbaric massacre and cold-blooded murder?"

"War mean fightin'; fightin' mean killin'..." Dobson recited, somewhat seethingly. "Ain't nuthin' more cold-blooded than that."

"Yes, well perhaps beyond the usual fog of war, the booze and the blood had shaded his soldier's eyes."

"I swear that debbil' Forrest thrived on blood and guts," Dobson said.

"Yes, a reputation for thriving on bloodshed can certainly intimidate your adversary," I concurred.

"You get inside a man's head," Dobson said.

"And to a man like Forrest, there was no means that was not worth the end. But perhaps he finally lost sight of the end. At least that is how he is judged."

"Massah' Forrest never worry 'bout being judged by the rest of us."

"By the rest of whom?" I wondered.

"By peoples who'd never seen humanity at its worst."

"What about you, George? You were there with Forrest. Have you ever worried about being judged for your role in the war?"

"Nope. I cain't say I ever studied it, Mister Herr Rommel."

I wasn't sure if I believed him, but once again I marveled at his penchant for making me contemplative and philosophical. "You know George, you enter war like another world and, while in it, judge your actions by that world's standards. But when it disappears in defeat, your actions are judged against all others, whether you worry about it or not."

"Yer' man Goethe?"

"That is my own," I tapped his baton against the bill of my hat.

"Mister Herr Rommel, I gots a question."

"What is it, George?"

"Why are you here?"

"To save my military career, George. I don't know if you heard, but in my last military campaign, I lost."

Perhaps still angry over his missing instrument, as a punitive gesture, Dobson said nothing.

"Now Mister Dobson, may I ask you a somewhat personal question?"

"Ain't that one already?"

"Perhaps it is."

"What do you wants to know, Mister Herr Rommel?"

"Well, your candid confessions about your encounter with the slave woman, the one who had been servicing General Forrest, made me wonder."

"Wonderin' what, exactly?"

"About your daughter Rosa, actually."

"Izzat right?"

"It is. Most specifically, it got me to wondering this: Does Rosa look more like you? Or more like General Forrest?"

Herr Dobson was at a loss for a response. He didn't quite know "how to act" without being able to slobber into that primitive mouth harp.

THE ATROCITIES

IN THE AFTERMATH OF FT. PILLOW, the trail of the Union dead was awe-inspiring. Hacked-up, brutalized bodies littered the landscape, beginning at the supply store, across the garrison, its artillery positions, the surrounding breastworks and into a river contaminated with gore. Floating corpses that continued to ooze blood exacerbated the discoloration of the river.

*****

In Meridian, Mississippi, Sherman was in his tent, reading aloud a telegraph from Grant.

"Grant says, 'Forrest must be driven out. Your preparations for the coming campaign must go on, but if it is necessary to detach a portion of the troops intended for it, detach them and make your campaign with that many fewer men. If a Greater Power does not effect judgment upon Forrest for the atrocities of Ft. Pillow, I leave it to you to enforce the same.'"

Sherman dropped his hands, still clutching the telegram. He dictated a reply to Grant.

"Adjutant, take this down to Grant. Tell him this: 'As if they needed more proof that the war is all but over, I have cut a swath of desolation fifty miles broad across the state of Mississippi, which the present generation will not forget.'"

Sherman affected an awkward pause.

"Is that all, sir?" The adjutant inquired.

"No, not quite. Tell Grant something he already knows. Tell him: 'That bastard Forrest is the rat in the meal barrel.'"

Grant and, by extension and hierarchical flow, Sherman, had to adjust their war strategy to not only contain uncertainty but also placate the Northern population, who had come to view Forrest as an instrument of the Devil, if not Mephistopheles himself. Indeed, newspaper headlines read: "MASSACRE AND GENOCIDE AT FT. PILLOW," and "THAT DEVIL FORREST OFFERS NO QUARTER FOR SURRENDERING UNION FORCES."

As a practical matter, as well as a public relations device, Forrest must be crushed—if not killed. To that end, Sherman sent Sturgis after the Wizard, to take command of the cavalry and, as he told Grant, "to whip Forrest, and, if necessary, to mount enough men to seize any and all the horses of Memphis, or wherever he may go. Forrest is insane and does not know the common sense of how a war should be fought. Fort Pillow has shown that Forrest is capable of anything. Kill Forrest and we will return to this country the unity upon which it was founded." Sherman was caught up in his own florid prose. He told Grant, in conclusion, that "We can give these poor niggers a taste of a life without chains. They may find that life on this mortal coil is bondage even without an overseer holding the whip. May the Good Lord have mercy on their simple, hapless souls."

BANTU

FOLLOWING DOBSON'S ACCOUNT of the Fort Pillow devastation, I was somewhat troubled by the blacksmith's lack of compassion for the slaughtered. As a military archivist and strategist, I had dismissed newspaper portrayals of Fort Pillow being a genocidal act as mere Northern propaganda. The victors write history, I would often surmise to myself. Strangely though, Dobson's description did very little to confirm my previous notions—and bias, perhaps—about Forrest as merely acting as a soldier in a difficult situation. It made me wonder if the victors and their agents of propaganda were not, in fact, right. As I pondered this, our car was somewhere between Guntown, Mississippi and Brice's Crossroads. And as the Lincoln crept closer to Brice's Crossroads, i.e., my—and maybe Dobson's—point of singularity, I was struck by the impotent landscape and how all these years later the cotton and the beans seemed to refuse to grow.

"At Fort Pillow his slave woman escaped?" I asked.

"I reckon she couldn't abide the killings anymore," Old Dobson told me. "Not when it was her own peoples."

"George, you asked me why I was here. Now let me ask you: Why were you here? Why didn't you desert?"

He said nothing. Instead, in response, he reached involuntarily for his jettisoned harmonica. He mimed playing. I was frustrated by his silence—if not insolence—and I stuck my baton between his clasped hands, into the reeds of his imaginary harp. He dropped his hands.

"Mr. Dobson," I wondered, "what ship did your *volks* come over on?"

"I been tolt' it was some slow boat out of Ghana."

"Hmmm... With my feeble knowledge of African geography and history, that means that you are.... Bantu."

"I reckon."

"Then your people were followers of Babatu Zoto."

"So I been tolt'."

"I thought so, Mr. Dobson. Your blood fought for a man that suffocated every tribe in Ghana. It is utterly atavistic. Like me and like General Forrest also, you are a warrior too."

"I prefers to think of myself as a blacksmith and a philosopher. Maybe even a humanis'. More so than a fighter. I fought for Massah Forrest because I had nowhere to go. Sherman burnt my home and left me with no place to hang my harp..."

I pointed at Dobson with the baton. "*Stierschiebe*," I said. "You fought for Forrest because it is what you do, George. War is in your blood. You come from a tribe of vicious slave traders. And you fought alongside a vicious slave trader. Mr. Dobson, as a warrior, with Forrest you were home. Only you fought with a hammer, not a spear."

I HAVE TRIED TO CONTAIN THAT MAN

CONFEDERATE STATES OF AMERICA PRESIDENT JEFFERSON DAVIS' OFFICE was littered with paperwork and scattered newspapers. He sifted through the same screaming headlines that grabbed Grant's attention. Furiously, Davis and Braxton Bragg perused the papers and tried to grasp the magnitude of the public relations disaster.

The President was beside himself. "The Northern papers are on fire with utter agitprop after this Fort Pillow debacle. 'Genocide,' they call it. 'Barbarians,' they call our Confederacy."

"President Davis," Bragg exclaimed, "I have tried to contain that man, but no matter the orders, he seems to follow his own agenda."

"Even so Bragg, he was right about the enemy's strategy at Shiloh, and he was right about The Union's vulnerability at Chattanooga. You did not listen then, much to the detriment of our cause. Am I supposed to listen to Forrest when he says Sherman is finished with Mississippi and is now going to take Atlanta? What do you think of this, Bragg?"

"Forrest is a loose cannon," Bragg mewled. "He cannot be trusted."

Jefferson Davis read aloud the contents of a message from Forrest. "'With our forces united a move could be made into Middle Tennessee and Kentucky which would create a diversion of the enemy's forces and enable us to break up Sherman's plans, and such an expedition, managed with prudence and executed with rapidity, can be safely made.'"

Davis caught his breath. "I put it to you, General Bragg: What if Forrest is right about Sherman's intentions and you are wrong?"

WE ARE GOING TO BE HIS RULER

THE LINCOLN ARRIVED QUIETLY at Brice's Crossroads. Inside, Ol' Dobson was asleep, cradling his flask and a roadmap.

"Herr Rommel, shall I wake the Schwarz, sir?" Schneider asked.

"Nein, nein. You may relax from your drive also, Schneider. I am going to wander and explore the battlefield for a while."

I exited the car and looked around the vacant, spectral battlefield. I took stock of the patches of battle debris half-grown over with amber and brown grass, and the railroad that lay in the close distance. Birds chirped as the wind blew across the plain. As I walked the forgotten battlefield, I closed my eyes and heard echoes of distant artillery and the yells of men engaged in combat. My face was solemn, but my soul was haunted—as was, perhaps, the soil upon which I stood.

"It was at this moment," I said to myself, "when, drunk from the carnage of Fort Pillow, Forrest conceived and executed his greatest military triumph."

As I walked, my imagination flashed back to artillery charges, exploding cannons and the rapid cackle of musketry. My eyes opened and I saw nothing but sun-bleached grass blowing in the azure wind. Closing my eyes again, I visualized the aftermath of battle and heard the wind blow and the flies buzz as they flitted and frolicked from a bounty of decaying, bloated corpses.

I knew this battle, and as I closed my eyes I projected to a spot five miles away from Brice's Crossroads, as Sturgis' black and white infantry marched on the double-quick through the wood to the field. The sweltering Mississippi summer heat and the wool uniforms of the Union soldiers acted as convection ovens. The men struggled with their personal effects, which they shed like hair on a dog. Breathing heavily and perspiring profusely, the Yanks managed to maintain the kind of vengeful spirit that trumps heat and discomfort. I could visualize Sturgis among them, suffering only a little less from being on horseback.

****

"Move up as rapidly as possible without distressing the troops," Sturgis commanded his infantry. "Make all haste. Lose no time coming up."

The perspiring soldiers continued to breathe heavily and ran towards the sound of battle.

"Five miles at double-quick. Criminy!" A union infantryman complained.

"Y'all white boys is soft," a Negro Union soldier teased. "Back on the plantation, I run this far jes' to be back in the slave quarters befo' the overseer wake up and find me in the sack with his woman."

The soldiers passed broken-down and tattered homes, some abandoned, and others with ladies fanning themselves silently on the porch like ghosts. The negro union soldier shook his fist at antebellum ladies on a farmhouse porch.

"We gwan' show Forrest we his rul-ah, ma'am," he declared. "We gwan' show that murderin' sumbitch' no quarter. Remembuh' Fort Pillow!"

The union men arrived at the battle site sun-struck and panting. Further dampening their spirit was the occasional retreating union cavalry rider.

TO PERPETUATE THE LIVING

AMONG FIELDS OF FULVOUS FLOWERS at Brice's Crossroads, I heard myself whisper, "*The firstest with the mostest...*"

I wandered into a meadow filled with a brook and more of the blooming flora and stumbled upon a collection of unmarked graves shaded from the sun by some pines and a smattering of magnolia trees. Yankees and Rebels, buried together, I surmised in silence. My deeply contemplative trance was broken by the sound of a harmonika echoing through the woods. This puzzled me, as my adjutant had jettisoned that odious instrument of Dobson's. Moreover, when I left him at the Lincoln, he seemed deep in a serious slumber. I began walking towards the source of what could loosely be called music. Then I heard what sounded like metal *auf* metal. I walked towards the sounds, pushing briars and tree branches aside. I heard more rustling and commotion, and finally found a pair of filthy white trash grave robbers. Sitting on a fresh mound from an unearthed grave was a bearded, scraggly man playing the harp. He wore ragged, gray wool clothes that were probably an old uniform liberated from a corpse. The other fellow had a shovel in his hands and a cigarette in his mouth. His face was filled with crags and his baked, withered skin was the color of the magnolia tree. He had one foot in a soldier's final resting place. His shovel would clang on the hinges of the dead man's casket. Next to the opened resting place laid a rifle, a dirty knapsack full of loot and a pair of soldier's boots. I made my presence felt and the shoveling and the music- making ceased.

"Didn't mean to interrupt your walk in the woods, Lieutenant," the grave robber said to me, flicking his cigarette.

"Nor I your revelry," I replied. "What are the spoils, if I may ask?"

"Found a dead man's colors and a harmon-a-kee for my cuz'n, here." The cousin showed me the instrument.

"And I just found me a blue belly's musket. Found me a pouch of Minié balls too. Good thing, too, cuz the woods been gettin' a might thick with squirrel."

The plunderer relieved the grave of the musket and patted the corpse down for more booty. Disappointed, he pulled out a knife and started to inspect the corpse's teeth, plying metal out of the dead man's teeth.

I was appalled. "My God, man! Have you no shame?"

"This here Billy Yank don't need no silver fillin's," the grave robber responded. "And he don't need no boots. The dead are only here to perpetuate the livin'. And the livin' need the dead like they need the wind and the sun and the rain. This soldier died the day the old ways were laid to rest so that a new nation could be born and I could have his musket."

As this necrotic ne'er-do-well ranted, the man in gray quietly resumed improvising on his harmonika. I became increasingly disgusted.

"You, sir, are attempting to justify your own barbarism and I will hear no more of such sophistry," I said, making my way towards the open grave.

"I seen your kind in Montfaucon in the Great World War, Herr Lieutenant."

"Perhaps."

"So you don't need me to tell you that nations are built on such sophistry," he said, as the harmonika music got louder. "And in accord with the principles of one Sir Isaac Newton, allow me to say that barbarism, like the Midas touch that turns precious metals into a projectile which will tear a hole in the human heart and cause these decaying corpses that make these perty' yeller flowers to grow—only to function as fodder for them varmints I'm gonna shoot with this here dead man's musket—can neither be created nor destroyed, but can only change form."

As he spoke, I wondered about the man's sanity. Had he actually been in France when I was there? It was all so surreal—made even more strange by the man's speech patterns and his cousin's curious musical notation, both of which were even more perplexing than Herr Dobson's. He continued his verbal effluvium: "After I finish here, I will be making my way with a modestly heavy heart warmed only by the comfort of knowing that these shoes and this musket will not only define, but indeed transcend the carbon cycle."

And with that, he stuck his knife in the dirt. As if to punctuate the gesture, the music stopped.

I began to scold the villain. "You are transcending nothing, you parasite. Your craven thievery besmirches the memory of a proud man who died for principles. Regardless of the color of his uniform, he died a patriot. Put his artifacts back in his grave."

The harmonika player whistled. "You hear that, Cuz'? This ol' boy says them Damn Yankees is patriots too!"

The grave robber snickered and shook a musket ball out of the pouch and began fiddling with his stolen rifle's muzzle. Despite the implied threat of the muzzle-loading, I stood my ground. The thief raised his voice even louder. "Remember, Herr Lieutenant, patriotism is not just the last refuge of a scoundrel—it is a necessary component of the circle of life. And in that circle, a nation is birthed only so it can die. You can fight for change, you can fight for things to stay the same, but it don't make no difference." The grave robber began to methodically load the musket with a ball, while his cousin doubled over in a laughing fit. "Firstest with the mostest, lastest with the leastest, whatever you're fighting for is fleeting, and will become fodder for worms soon enough, whether you fight for it or not." With the musket loaded with the Minié ball, the bandit leveled the rifle and pointed it at my face.

"You are utterly deranged swine."

"Now that may be. But that is a nice piece of decoration swingin' 'round your neck. I'd be most obliged if you were to part with that fine pendant."

"That is my Blue Max. Many men died in Italy so I could wear it."

"And another man will die so's I can wear it. Either way possession is temporary. Just ask Billy Yank here."

And with that he lowered his head, closed one eye and pulled the trigger. There was a puff of blue smoke and then nothing. Perhaps due to its age and rot, the musket misfired. I tried not to flinch. Both the hooligans laughed and the digger began to prime the barrel for another ball. "Looks like you gotta head start," he laughed. Then there was another shot—and the grave robber dropped his pilfered weapon. Blood gushed out of the redneck's forehead. Stunned, his cousin dropped his harp. I turned to my right—towards the source of the sound of the shot—and Schneider coolly locked eyes with mine. He blithely waved a smoking Luger pistol. The sounds of twigs snapping and leaves crackling broke our stare.

Through the foliage, we could see the skinny man in the ragged wool uniform skip and jump like a doe. Schneider fired two shots, and missed as the dead redneck's accomplice kept running. My adjutant then put his pistol in its holster, under his trench coat.

"I'll finish here, Herr Lieutenant," he said, removing the bandit's knife from its perch in the soil. As I walked back towards the highway I heard him kick the fresh corpse into the hole that had just been dug up by the newly deceased. Then I heard shoveling. I always felt Schneider was a dutiful if not magnificent soldier, if not a marginal shot.

I reached the Lincoln just as Ol' Dobson awakened from his nap. Rubbing my forehead, I cleared the disgust with my previous encounter as a doddering Dobson clumsily climbed out of the car. As the grass and the flowers blew, we stood in silence, our bodies absorbing gusts of wind.

"Hey man," Dobson yawned. "What was all that yellin'?"

I wasn't sure how to answer. "For all its supernatural myth and majesty, there is still a lot of living evil at these crossroads, Herr Dobson."

Moments later we were joined by Schneider. As we entered the sedan, he casually tossed the dead man's knife and his cousin's pilfered harmonika onto the vacant passenger seat.

"Here you go, blind man," Schneider said. "Play some more of your simple music."

"Mercy sakes," Dobson explained. "Y'all found my harp."

"It's a different harp," Schneider insisted. After he gave the instrument of euphony to our tour guide, he put the instrument of blood in the Lincoln's glove box.

EVERYTHING FORWARD AT ONCE

INSIDE A TATTERED TENT, Morton and Forrest avoided the sweltering sun. Its thick, punishing heat compelled Forrest to remove his wool coat and mop his brow. In a fit of vanity, Forrest groomed himself, brushing the thick locks, clipping nose hairs, and trimming eyebrows while Morton went over papers. He suddenly stopped his preening mid-stroke and set down his mirror.

"What is it, General?" Morton inquired.

"Yankees," Forrest announced, rising. "And lots of 'em."

"Is it a battle?"

"It will be a battle soon enough," Forrest declared. "Sturgis wants me hit his center at Guntown Road, but I never took a dare from them yet, and won't do it today."

"What do you propose, sir?"

"We're going to fight them on our terms… and on our terrain. And we shall hit them on the end…"

"Sir?"

"Come on!" Forrest exhorted.

Forrest walked briskly toward the front line as soldiers were dressing and preparing artillery for the battle, which could be heard in the background. Morton kept pace with him.

"Sturgis is on the move, but I have a mind not to face his guns."

"Not to face them, sir? But I though you said…"

"Not to face them," Forrest explained, "but go around them. Tell Bell to move forward and fetch all he's got."

"Yes, sir!"

Morton ran off. In the background, battle became louder. A roaring huzzah sounded from the Confederates and Forrest smiled.

✶✶✶✶✶

My face shared Forrest's bliss. "Mr. Dobson, how are you feeling?" I asked.

"Right as rain, Lieutenant."

"Come, let us walk to Tishomingo Creek."

*****

CSA soldiers fell to the ground for rest and laid panting in the dense heat, under the shade of trees. In shirtsleeves, Forrest rode up on horseback.

"Get up, men," Forrest enjoined. "I have ordered Bell to charge on the left. When you hear his guns, and the bugle sounds, every man must charge and we will give them hell."

The Men were hot and exhausted and somewhat dazed. Forrest continued his pep talk.

"Men of the Tennessee Cavalry Battalion you have shown indomitable spirit and will, but goddammit, this is no occasion to waver. We are outnumbered by their two to our one and any military textbook will tell you that you must attack with a superior force of three men to their every one. But those are only numbers! For the Tennessee Cavalry to triumph, I need each man to attack. There will be no skulking! I will shoot you myself if you are afraid the Yanks might hit you. I will lead you!"

"Huzzah!" the soldiers whooped in unison.

****

I closed my eyes and whispered, "This was his time. He ordered the military forward, everything forward at once."

"Yes suh," Dobson confirmed. "Everything forward at once."

****

"There will be no feints," Forrest shouted. "It will be a charge up the middle and two charges on either flank. We will hit 'em in the middle and we will hit on the *e-e-e-n-d!* At every point, we must get there firstest with the mostest!"

Forrest continued pointing and shouting encouragement. Cannons were pushed forward by hand, under the direction of Morton.

"General!" Morton implored. "Isn't it folly to throw our guns forward without support?"

"Morton, all the Yankees in front of us cain't get to your guns."

Yankee officers dropped their swords mid-order and deserted. Sturgis, on horseback, grabbed at a man, held his terrorized, shamed face and then let go.

"Everything at the crossroads is going to the devil as fast as it possibly can," Sturgis muttered to himself.

On foot, the cavalry charged through the brush. Hand to hand fighting ensued. Spent rifles were used as clubs; pistols fired while the two lines struggled with the ferocity of wild beasts. Forrest raised his saber and pointed it at Lt. Cowan. "The time has come to hit 'em on the *e-e-e-end*!" he shouted.

LIKE A THUNDER CLOUD

I LOOKED TOWARDS THE WOODS AND SMILED.

"We shadowed Sturgis the whole time—like a black cloud," Dobson remembered. "Then lightnin' struck."

"Jawohl, jawohl. Lightning strikes… *die blitzkrieg…*"

Pointing to a bridge, I asked: "It was there, wasn't it? Where all three points of attack coalesced. At Tishomingo Creek."

"Yep," Herr Dobson said. "We put the squeeze on 'em at Tishomingo Crick and when them Blue Bellies got the fear, they forgot they wuz' soldiers. Our cavalry chased 'em through the forest and hunted 'em down like a pack of hounds."

ALL THE WAY TO MEMPHIS

STURGIS' MEN CONTINUED TO FLEE. Their egress mirrored their ingress as the aforementioned Negro Union soldier once again shook his fist at the same gathering of ladies on the Reverend Agnew's porch. The ladies jeered back at him.

"That debbil' Forrest may have today," the retreating Negro Union soldier declared. "But he still gwan pay for Fort Pillow, ma'am."

Amidst the chaos, a wagon train attempted to turn around. The lead wagon capsized and fell into the creek. The remaining wagons and an artillery train were abandoned. Like locusts, the CSA soldiers fed on the goods that poured from the capsized wagon and slashed the canvas of the other carriages while stuffing themselves and their pockets full of food and goods.

The night was on fire. Many of Forrest's triumphant cavalry lighted their pursuit of the retreating Yankees with torches. Forrest rode through the foreground.

"Keep the skeer on 'em," Forrest shouted. "All the way to Mem'fus."

SOLDIER'S JOY

ON THE OUTSKIRTS OF MEMPHIS, a southbound train puffed slowly and ground to a halt, squeaking its brakes until reaching the scene of Sturgis' retreat. Beyond dark windows, women sighed and whined as the steam billowed and the chugging ceased.

Forrest was suddenly accosted by a barrage of close shots and dived into a car, six-shooter in one hand and his bloody saber in the other.

The darkened train car was filled with about twenty rows of weary prostitutes. Some of the ladies screamed. Forrest burst into the cabin with his pistol and a bloody saber drawn.

"Good evening, ladies," he charmed.

"Why Gen'ruh. You give us a fright," a prostitute with a missing tooth declared.

Periodic bursts of artillery and torches lit up Forrest's determined glare. With a bloodied rag, he wiped his saber, then his brow.

"You fine specimens of virtue must be Joe Hooker's girls," he marveled.

"We ain't nobody's girls in particular," one of the whores volunteered, "but I could be your girl, you handsome devil."

"Back in Virginia," another girl hooted, "we wuz' General Hooker's girls, until he got his bell rung. Now we're working under the Army of the Tennessee!"

"Which Army of the Tennessee?" Forrest asked.

"Why the victorious Army of the Tennessee, of course," the Missing Tooth snorted.

"I see," Forrest chortled. "Merely abiding the whims of supply and demand, ladies?"

"Why, General!" one of the girls teased. "How do you find the supply?"

"Ample. The supply is ample, but the demand is soon to wither and shrink. You may have noticed that there is a war going on and my men are here to ensure you will be working under the Confederates.

"Suh," purred one trollop. "I've always had a weakness for the Southern gentleman."

"Madame," Forrest replied, "if we weren't in the midst of battle I would consider introducing you to that famous Southern charm now. But if you will excuse me."

"Be sure and come back when you can stay longer, Gen'ral." the girls laughed.

With a flourish he lifted his cap towards the ladies who smiled and giggled. As he began to exit the train, he flashed them a dashing grin while perusing the assembled. In the second row, four feet from where he was standing, sat Catharine in a gaudy, revealing dress. She stared at him blankly. He looked at her, and his smile disappeared. Breaking the stalemate, Forrest nodded his head stoically before leaping back into the battle, his exit followed by hollers of support from the painted ladies. As the women chattered about the virility of the Southern men and the size of their sabers, Catharine looked away.

Outside, among the detritus of war, another Federal wagon in Forrest's path was capsized. He watched with glee as his soldiers seized upon it as they had the others.

NO SOBER MAN

SHERMAN DICTATED a telegraph as his adjutant scribbled diligently.

"I am of the opinion that Sturgis is losing his grip," he recited. "His reports say that Forrest had 20,000 men to our 8,000. In reality, it appears that Forrest had only 4,000 men and was able to whoop Sturgis with far inferior numbers. I am now of the opinion that Sturgis was drunk. No sober man can get his ass beaten that badly."

*****

OUTSIDE THE LINCOLN, I heard and felt the ghosts of the dead from the Battle of Brice's Crossroads. Herr Dobson sat on the right front fender and ended our silent contemplation by playing the blues on his harmonica.

"Once you hear the details of victory," I said, "it is hard to distinguish it from a defeat."

Dobson put down the harmonica. "You gots to read the fine print, Lieutenant. This weren't no victory. This wasn't a tick on a dog's dick."

I disagreed with the Negro. "But Forrest triumphed under daunting circumstances and impossible odds. He persevered, winning a Pyrrhic victory in a lost war."

"Sherman just wanted to keep Forrest busy so he could march to the sea unmolested and burn down Atlanta," Herr Dobson declared. "Sherman turned everything in his path into smoldering ruins. Burned every house and every barn and kilt the crops and blowed up the rails and took the livestock and salted the wells. Just like he did to the Montgomerys in Eighteen Hunnerd and Sixty-One. Then tolt the black folks that they was free, but to stay away from his white ass, cuz' he didn't owe them nuthin'."

"But he liberated them. He made them free."

"Free to what?" Dobson cried, and stood up. "Pound sand? Eat they mules?"

Dobson opened the car door and rooted around the interior for his flask.

"Are you saying they preferred slavery?" I must admit my head was somewhat spinning. "Or that they even enjoyed their servitude?"

"I ain't sayin' shit," Ol' Dobson said, while removing the top of the bottle. "I'm sayin' Sherman was free to burn people's shit like Attila the Hun. And Forrest was free to fuck around and wipe out a buncha nigger soldiers at Fort Pillow who was dumb enough to think that they wuz' free. At best, they wuz' at they crossroads. At worst, they wuz' just cannon fodder as Forrest was makin' a fool of a simple man like Sturgis."

"But they... you wuz'... were... ARE... free," I suggested.

"Yes suh, Lieutenant. Every bit as free as you is. Maybe freer. I chose my master. Same as you."

Dobson spat and offered me the flask. I swallowed and winced.

"Jawohl, jawohl. Perhaps freedom is beyond our grasp... like glory, like all constructs be they human or holy, freedom is a lie or at the very least, fleeting."

"Sho' nuff," Ol' Dobson concurred. "If'n glory and freedom is just passin' through, you gots' to ask yourself, Herr Lieutenant: Was it all worth it?"

With a start, my head jerked as if slapped by a ghost. A sharp wind gusted in my face. I took another drink.

ONE ROAD TO HELL

NASHVILLE IN DECEMBER. 1864. It was bitterly cold. Forrest's soldiers were dressed in a motley assortment of gray and captured blue uniforms. This once-proud, now-ramshackle and unkempt collection of soldiers were on foot, fighting for survival. Cannon shells exploded and blew holes in the Rebel lines. For the first time, their faces were red with fear. Forrest was overcome and had tears streaming down his face.

"Rally, men, rally," Forrest implored. "For God's sake, rally!"

In a pushed contrast to their earlier allegiance at earlier battles, the barefoot and tattered infantry ignored their leader. It was pandemonium. The color-bearer himself ran past Forrest on his way out of the fighting.

"Halt!" Forrest screeched.

The color bearer continued to flee. Forrest took his pistol and shot him. Forrest gathered the flag, but the panicked infantry ignored the gesture and refused to rally around it, continuing their flight.

Forrest fired at random, hitting nothing. Young Dobson suddenly appeared next to him as Forrest reached the height of panic, pistol in one hand, flag in the other.

"Gen'ruh Forrest!" Dobson cried, "Gen'ruh Forrest! Knock that shit off! It's done nah…"

In his mania, Forrest pointed the pistol at Young Dobson's head, then stopped himself and lowered it. Young Dobson didn't flinch.

"It's over, Massah Forrest. I'm goin' home. You should go home, too."

Young Dobson turned and walked away. The Confederate defense continued to crumble. In full flight, a panicked officer ran by, fleeing with his troops.

"Halt!" Forrest commanded.

Forrest hurled the flag at the officer's head. It darted through the air, its stars and bars stiffening for a moment, and then fell to the ground, a meaningless, bullet-ridden rag. In the background Young Dobson watched the spectacle and turned his horse and wagon.

Gaus continued to issue the charge, but his bugle was shot from his mouth.

*****

LATER THAT WINTER, after the ignominious defeat at Nashville, on the outskirts of Memphis, a bedraggled Forrest and Morton stopped their less-than-impressive steeds at a fork in the road. Only a handful of soldiers, mostly in rags or gurneys and all with downtrodden, bloody faces followed.

"Which road, General?" Morton asked.

"It makes no difference," Forrest mused. "If one road led to hell and the other to Mexico, I wouldn't care which one I took."

ONLY THE VANQUISHED

BACK IN OUR LINCOLN, we headed east, toward the airfield in Memphis.

"After Sherman torches the homes of thousands of innocent civilians, your government wants to try Forrest for his role in the so-called War Crimes at Fort Pillow?" I asked.

"Yes, 'suh, Herr Lieutenant. Everyone be complicit. Only the vanquished be guilty of War Crimes."

"Yes, yes. And only the vanquished start secret societies."

"You mean dem' Ku Klux?"

"*Jawohl.*"

"What do you know about dem' Ku Klux?"

The Lincoln motored through the Delta towards Memphis. The swastikas danced in the shadows of cedar trees and Spanish moss.

FORREST KNELT

AFTER THE WAR, in Memphis' town square, much of the populace milled around, having heard that the Ku Klux Klan would be demonstrating. It was mostly white families, flanked by some curious black folks standing in the back. There was a subdued hush as a muffled sound was heard from the direction of the road out of town. At the bend the glow of candles in the dark multiplied as some two-hundred men in white robes, their horses also dressed in white, with cloth wrapped around their hooves to muffle the clop, filed in. Men, women and children stood in awe on the walkways. The black families were horrified.

Later, in the woods outside of Memphis, Forrest and Captain Morton rode on horseback. They slowed as they noticed torchlight among the trees. Morton led Forrest into the clearing where about fifteen men clad in Klan hoods stood in a ceremonial circle, their torches lighting Forrest's somber face.

He knelt and was knighted by one of the hooded men.

TWENTY-NINE HORSES AND THIRTY YANKEES

"THE SUB-COMMITTEE CALLS Mr. Nathan Bedford Forrest," a senate leader summoned.

Forrest walked with some difficulty to a seat behind a desk facing a committee of six senators.

The Senator noticed Forrest walking with difficulty. "I am surprised you can still put one foot in front of the other, for a man who wuz shot five times during the War."

Forrest laughed, "You mean the Recent Unpleasantness." The assembled chortled and guffawed. "Yes suh. If only our poor horses didn't get the brunt of it. Them Yanks musta' killed a score of my horses, if I'm a day old."

"By collating the battle reports from both sides," the Senator figured, "most reporters from Harpers put the number at twenty-nine."

"It was twenty-nine?" Forrest deadpanned. "Ah Senator, you Billy Yanks always did seem to know more than you let on."

"The same newspaper states that you personally killed thirty Union soldiers."

Forrest beamed. "Twenty-nine horses and thirty Yankees? I reckon I ended up one ahead."

The assembled came unglued with laughter.

"Yes." the Senate leader shushed. "Well perhaps the moment is nigh for this committee to explore your activities after the war."

"I cannot speak of anything personally," Forrest explained, "and my only knowledge of the existence of any such order as the Ku Klux is information from others."

Later, Forrest explained that he "lied like a gentlemen."

A HULLABALOO ERUPTS

"WELL THEN," THE SENATE LEADER WONDERED, "in regards to their existence, will you enlighten the Committee as best you can in detail?"

"Yes suh, well the organization did exist in 1866 and 1867," Forrest recalled, "right after the war, although I cannot be sure exactly what it was called. Some called them Pale Faces; some the Ku Klux. I had joined the Pale Faces in Memphis in 1867 but that was a different order from this, more something like Odd Fellowship, Masonry, orders of that sort."

"So this was a social club?" This inspired chuckles all around. "Sir, could you tell us more about the Pale Faces? Have you seen a copy of their constitution?"

"I confess that I have, suh," Forrest confirmed. "But I was more interested in raising money for the reconstruction and didn't involve myself too much in all of it."

"Raise money for what exactly?"

"Oh railroads, public buildings, things of that sort."

"The very railroads you tore up in your raids on the Federal Army?"

"It's hard to say who tore up more, me or Sherman," Forrest quipped, stirring laughter from the assembled.

"So this club was an instrument of reconstruction?"

"And an implement of defense."

"Defense of what?" The Senate leader was incredulous.

"What was left of our way of life," Forrest intoned. "Between the carpetbaggers, the scalawags and the niggers getting' the vote, a white man couldn't even pull himself up by his bootstraps. It was a goddamned Yankee occupation."

"So to clarify, Mr. Forrest. You're saying that your Ku Klux Klan was an instrument of defense? That was the purpose of this organization?"

Forrest paused. "If a man took your gavel and beat you with it, would you call that justice? Or would you break it in half so he couldn't beat you with it any longer? The purpose? It was, I would say, for self-protection from Yankees who didn't realize the War was supposed to be over."

A hullabaloo erupted from this statement that was interrupted by the bang of a gavel. The Senators shuffled papers and grumbled to calm themselves. Forrest sat calmly.

"Mr. Forrest," the Senate leader concluded, "this committee would like to know how you can justify the violence that has continuously occurred around you, that you seem to at the very least condone."

Forrest paused again. "We all must do what we got to do to get by."

CRAZY ASS FLAGGE

WE CONCLUDED our drive through the Delta. Back in Memphis, we arranged to meet the Ford Motor Company man at the airfield, and because of Schneider's yeoman-like driving we appeared to be on time to keep our engagement. In the interim, we continued our small talk with Herr Dobson sharing his theories on how the Ku Klux Klan dealt with Federal forces during the years following the War.

"If your house be occupied," Dobson said, "you best make some noise and act like a ghost. Spook the livin' shit out of the carpetbaggers and make 'em rue the day they entered your property. Least ways, that's how it started."

"Ideologies and good intentions often get perverted and distorted, George."

"I reckon it seemed like a good idea at the time."

At the airfield, I engaged the Ford representative. Schneider unloaded the luggage from the car and stacked it on a cart. He was visibly relieved that the drive was over and made small talk to himself in German.

I shook Ol' Dobson's hand. "Thank you for your guidance and expertise, Herr Dobson. It has been... informative."

"Us type folks appreciate the ride, Lieutenant. Gave me a chance to visit some ghosts I had to say good riddance to."

"Well, as we say, *auf weidershen*. I would like to grace you with a keepsake from the Fatherland. I would like you to have our flag as a memento of our journey."

"Thanks all the same," Dobson declared, "but I just as soon you keep your keepsake. Every time white folks hand me some crazy ass flag, there is hell to pay."

"Ja, Ja. Very understandable sentiments. Perhaps I can offer you the baton?"

"You can keep that too, Lieutenant. I got nuthin' to point at and no mo' battles to fight."

"There must be something I can bequeath to you as a token of esteem and appreciation?"

"I reckon they' is. You forgettin' maybe the rest of the foldin' money?"

"Oh yes, of course. The balance of five hundred moon pies. Schneider, pay the man."

"*Danke*, Herr Schneider." The Negro saluted.

"And Mr. Dobson," the man in the black suit interjected, "you will remember to keep the details of this trip between us."

"I reckon that even more than the money, a reminder of the great emancipator proclaimater will keep me quiet as a Mississippi mudpuppy."

"The what will keep you what?" the man from Ford asked.

"He wants your sedan," I translated.

"This heah' Lincoln will keep my mouth shut." Dobson confirmed.

And the deal was struck.

THE DEVIL IS MY FRIEND

IN FLIGHT, I jotted down notes and mused on my experience in the delta and hill country of Mississippi. I looked out of the window at Memphis and the Mississippi River. I felt a little feverish—perhaps the cumulative effects of our travels in the wet, torrid heat of the Deep South. My eyes felt heavy and fluttered involuntarily, so I opened them wide and looked outside the airplane window as we passed over Memphis, Tennessee.

To my astonishment, thousands of feet below in the middle of the town square, I had a chimeric vision of a dandified Forrest in what appeared to be the post-war years. I saw a 4th of July celebration in full effect on a dusty, busy city block. As a steam engine puffed smoke, bands marched and played and pyrotechnics whistled, screamed and exploded. I was no longer on the airplane looking out, but on the city street itself.

It appeared to me that this was a particularly poignant Independence Day, as freed slaves nervously yet defiantly intermingled with former plantation owners, belles and dandies. The collective mood was torn between jubilation, emancipation, celebration, muted hatred and resignation.

On a wooden stage, a banner read: July Fourth, 1875, under which a feeble, gray Nathan Bedford Forrest accepted a bouquet of flowers from a blushing light-skinned Negress. He looked far more decrepit than I had ever imagined him—my guess was that the post-war years took their toll on his health and his psyche, the debilitation transpiring on an accelerated curve. Was this because of all the gunshot wounds? The stress of battle? Or the soul-crushing weight and pressure of an existential guilt?

As the hoary Forrest prepared to deliver a speech to an audience of the Jubilee Of Pole Bearers, onstage a Negress welcomed him. "Mr. Forrest," she said, "allow me to present you with this bouquet as a token of reconciliation, an offering of peace and good will." She curtsied.

Forrest bowed. "Miss Lewis, Ladies and Gentlemen," he nodded, "I accept these flowers as a token of reconciliation between the white and colored races in the South. I accept these more particularly, since they came from a colored lady, for if there is any one on God's green earth who loves the ladies, it is myself."

Nervous laughter emitted from the assembled and cut some of the racial tension. Among those chuckling was someone I assumed to be the Young Dobson. As the laughter subsided, a whistling firework climbed in pitch to a piercing crescendo, startling the crowd. When the assembled realized it was merely a firework and not a gun, the merriment resumed. Among the jovial was a woman with a weathered countenance and ragged couture of a tattered prostitute—this must have been Catharine. Forrest squinted his weathered eyes when he thought he saw both Young Dobson and Catharine. He shook his head to dispel the vision and returned his attention to the speech.

"This is a proud day for me," Forrest continued. "Having occupied the position I have for thirteen years and being misunderstood by the colored race, I take this occasion to say that I am your friend. I am here as a representative of the southern people. I want to elevate every man, and see that you take your places in your shops, stores and offices. I feel that you are free men, I am a free man, and we can do as we please."

Members of the crowd, mostly black, listened while fanning themselves impatiently. A woman played with the child on her lap. Blinded by the sun, Forrest took a beat and attempted to gather his sensibilities. People coughed. Onstage, Miss Lewis beamed, pink with pride, oblivious to the awkward silence.

"I assure you," Forrest resumed, "that every man who was in the Confederate Army is your friend. We were born on the same soil, breathe the same air, live on the same land. Why should we not be brothers and sisters?"

Bedford squinted. He looked broken.

"When the war broke out," Forrest said, "I believed it was my duty to fight for my country, and I did so. I will do all I can to bring harmony, peace and unity to our country."

A black man in the crowd insisted this trope was twaddle. "Wuz you our friend when you started that there Ku Klux?"

Red with irritation, Forrest calmed himself. "Even when I was wrong," he said, "I have always stood for what is right. I was right then and I am right now."

The crowd grew a little rowdy. The Negroes argued amongst themselves about the worth and character of the man in front of them. Young Dobson grinned and seemed to be enjoying the dissension among the assembled. Rosa poked Young Dobson in the ribs and smiled.

"I come here as a friend!" Forrest exulted. "I come here as a friend and whenever I can serve any of you, I will do so. We have one Union, one flag and one country, therefore let us stand together. I thank you for the flowers and assure you that I am with you in heart and hand."

As the audience applauded, I saw Rosa make eye contact with Catharine, who looked back, apparently pleased to see Rosa with Ol' Dobson.

"Well I'll be," he chuckled. "The debbil be my friend." Then he spat.

*****

A mile high in the sky, the propellers of the passenger plane whirred. I slept, my notebook and pen still in my hands. In my dreams, I realized Rosa was the offspring of Herr Dobson and Forrest's mistress.

BACK ON TERRA FIRMA

BACK ON TERRA FIRMA, the sun began its descent and the Model K rambled down the road with Ol' Dobson at the wheel. Sticking his hand out of the window, he waved at our airplane.

"Auf wiedersehen, Herr Lieutenant!" He yelled, taking a hit off of his flask and shook his head.

"How you gonna act, you crazy cracker motherfucker?" he said, as he grabbed the wretched grave robber's harmonica out of the car's glove box and began wailing away as the Lincoln rolled on.

"How you gonna act?" he sang.

SWORN TO SECRECY

WITH THE SWASTIKAS BUFFETING on the Lincoln's fenders, Mr. Dobson continued to drive southeast across the Mississippi delta. It was night, but the man with one-eye drove with his sunglasses still on. To the south, across a muddy cotton field, a twelve-foot cross was on fire.

Parked cars with their lights on served as a crossroads barricade. Menacing hooded figures bearing torches flanked the cars and forced Dobson to stop. A Klansman approached. A skinny man in ragged wool clothes accompanied him. Behind them, the assembled gathered.

"Boy," the Klansman said. "Wha... Why you drivin' in the dark with sunglasses on?"

"I reckon I'm used to makin' my way in the dark," Dobson answered.

"You wanna tell how 'n the hell a half-blind nigra' came to own this fine ahh-to-mo-beel?"

"I can't rightly say," Ol' Dobson said, the light of the burning cross reflected in his shades. "I be sworn to secrecy by agents of the gov'ment."

"You best be talkin', boy."

"If I was pressed for an answer, it be a gift from the future, I reckon."

"There was a killin' tonight at Brice's Crossroads. And word is this big' ol' car was there."

"I don't know shit about anybody dying at Brice's Crossroads. Not since 1864, anyway."

The skinny man had enough of Dobson's evasive answers. "This sho' is the car that them that kilt my cousin drove up in at the crossroads. And that there," he exclaimed, reaching into the breast pocket of the black man's overalls, "is sho' nuff' the harp he found."

As the mob of hooded figures gathered to extricate the old man from the Lincoln, Dobson uttered his last words of defiance: "Hey, you motherfuckin' Ku Klux! Gimme back my harp!"

REALM OF DUSK (1942)

AS I HAD EXPECTED IN POTSDAM, before my trip to America's Deep South, war had indeed come to pass. I was prepared, however—I had taken Forrest's tactics and written a thesis applying his cavalry maneuvers to tank warfare. Subsequently, the Chancellor promoted me from Lieutentant to Field Marshall.

In North Africa, on the simmering southern shores of the Mediterranean Sea, I raised my binoculars and attempted to make sense of the swirling fans of desert dunes. In a maelstrom of blood, motor oil, grinding wheels, sand, snot and tank tracks, blond, blue-eyed sunburned men were mowed down and chewed up like gristle in a series of slow industrial accidents. As a tactician and Field Marshall, I must admit, I was rather indifferent to the suffering.

The wind blew sand and I wiped my eyes. It wasn't supposed to be this difficult but Berlin had insisted on splitting the Reich's firepower and manpower into two fronts, on separate continents, making the strategic deployment of arms and bodies half as efficient and twice as bloody.

My troops were pummeled, but they continued an inexorable march into the shape-shifting sands of utter annihilation.

"Hit them on the end!" I ordered, but my famed pincer strategy— one I had developed from years of study and my journey to Brice's Crossroads—cut no muster on a battlefield soft as marshmallows.

It all turned to dross. Disorientation was situation normal: Infantry immolated and Panzers pummeled. The desert heat, the fumes, the bone-shivering bombardment, the earth torn asunder. I wiped my eyes again with a gloved hand, disbelievingly.

Still trying to gauge the size, strength and position of my foe, I looked through my glass once more and the dust parted just long and wide enough to create a hole in my consciousness. I shook my head. I could not believe what I saw: The Allied forces were not in tanks, but were on instruments from a forgotten century. The opponents were men on horses. It made no sense; I was looking at a mirage. It was Yankee cavalry. From another century. From the American Civil War. "Hit 'em on the end!" I repeated, oblivious to the absurdity of the hallucination.

At that moment, I knew it was hopeless. I had failed to absorb the lessons of Brice's Crossroads: those lessons that Dobson had pointed out to me, even the messages of that psychotic, homicidal gravedigger. Here in North Africa, I attempted a most ambitious pincer movement, not unlike the attack that Forrest had foisted on the hapless Sturges in Mississippi, but mine was on a meta-scale: I would take Forrest's approach and apply it as a radical, far-reaching invasion from Cairo to the Caucasians; in one sweeping gesture, take out the Allied Forces in the desert as well as the nefarious Russians in the east. But like Forrest's conquest at the Crossroads, my fight was Pyrrhic at best. Unlike Forrest's, it wasn't even a victory. It was unsustainable, and dare I say it was also untenable—which was what the Negro and the grave digger were both telling me—beware of sophists and their charisma and its inevitable end: barbarism. To be more blunt, beware of the Chancellor.

This epiphany forced me to curse in an unguarded moment, with my field glasses pressed against my face.

"Scheiße," I muttered.

"Vas is Das, Field Marshall?" an adjutant inquired.

"Sherman," I exhaled.

"American Sherman tanks?"

"Nein. It is worse that that," I muttered, lowering the glass again. "William 'Tecumseh' Sherman."

"Scheiße," the adjutant mumbled.

CHARRED AND MANGLED (1944)

THE MUTE TRANQUILITY of a remote military bunker in a German forest was shattered by a ferocious explosion that rocked the foundation of the building. As a door swung open, charred and mangled Third Reich military men fought their way amidst billowing smoke and burning papers. The intended victim of the terrorist explosion, the Chancellor, survived.

I wasn't there that day—and perhaps my absence only pointed to my complicity.

BUSINESS

DAYS AFTER THE BOMB BLAST, I heard a noise outside my study, parted the curtains and noticed a black Mercedes Benz coupe parked by a garden gate inside the compound of my home. I saw that Schneider sat in the driver's seat. As a German shepherd barked, General Burgdorf and General Maisel—my former subordinates—knocked at the front door of the Lieutenant's residence.

My lovely wife, Lucia, greeted Burgdorf and Maisel at the door.

"Frau Rommel," Burgdorf enjoined.

"Herr Burgdorf, Herr Maisel. Heil Hitler!"

"Heil Hitler," Burgdorf and Maisel chanted in unison.

"The attempt on his life was unthinkable," Lucia proffered. "What absolute horror."

"Most unfortunate," Burgdorf agreed. "And ill-advised."

"What an inspired miracle that he was able to walk away unharmed from a bomb placed at his feet," Lucia intoned.

"His survival was no miracle," Burgdorf contended. "The Fuhrer's indomitable spirit and will shall triumph any attempts at subverting the Reich."

"Begging pardon, Frau Rommel," Maisel chimed, "but we have business with Field Marshall Rommel."

"Jawohl, of course. He has been expecting you. Please, let me take to you his study."

Uniformed in an open-collared African tunic, I was in conversation with my blond 15-year old son, Manfred. He too heard the car drive up and was aware of the visitors before the knock on my study door.

"So, today will decide what is planned for me, Manfred," I warned.

"You would accept such a command?" Manfred asked.

"My dear Manfred, our enemy in the East is so terrible that every other consideration has to give way before it. If Stalin succeeds In conquering Europe, even only temporarily, it will be the end of every thing that makes life appear worth living. Of course I will go."

It was then that Frau Lucia knocked on the door of the study and poked her head in.

"Darling," Lucia interrupted, "Generals Burgdorf and Maisel are here on business."

"Of course, Lucia, of course. Show them in."

As Manfred excused himself, Burgdorf and Maisel exulted "Heil Hitler!" simultaneously.

"Heil Hitler," Manfred returned, and as Manfred and Lucia took their leave, I offered the men libations.

"Brandy?"

"No," Burgdorf declined. "This is no social visit."

"Nein?"

"We are here to execute the Fuhrer's orders," Maisel explained.

"As military men, aren't we all?

"Not unless sedition and treachery are among his desires," Burgdorf warned.

I knew what they were referring to, but appeared puzzled. "Sedition?"

"Yes, Field Marshall" Burgdorf confirmed. "Say covert attempts at establishing peace and signing treaties with Eisenhower.

"Perhaps while annihilating Der Fuhrer?" added Maisel.

"I have always defended the Fatherland and will die with its best interests at heart," I insisted. "A wizened man once explained to me that the only contract a man has to honor is the deal he makes in his heart."

The Generals were unmoved. "Der Fuhrer says that in view of your services in Africa you may die quickly and efficiently by poison," Burgdorf said. "It is fatal in three seconds. If you accept, none of the usual steps will be taken against your family."

"You will spare my family a life of forced labor?"

"Yes," Maisel answered. "They are hardly mongrels."

"You will receive a hero's burial," Burgdorf reported.

"Why bother?" I asked. "There is no room for sentimentality in war."

With gravel crunching under their jackboots, Burgdorf, Maisel and I walked out of the house towards the Mercedes parked by the garden gate. A gathering of villagers stood outside the drive. My German shepherd resumed barking ferociously.

Schneider opened the passenger door and stood to attention. The Generals raised their right hands in salute. Burgdorf moved aside for me to enter the car. I pushed my marshal's baton under my left arm, and placidly gave my wife and son a farewell salute.

A little further down the road, Schneider brought the black Mercedes Benz to a halt at the edge of some woods.

With the motor off, Schneider stood next to the car nervously and smoked. Gestapo soldiers rushed the silent vehicle with guns drawn. The show of arms struck me as pointless as my resistance was non-existent. Schneider opened the passenger door and my marshal's baton fell from my hand and hit the pavement.

Upon my baton's impact, I could not help but remember my old tour guide and marvel at the irony of how we were killed by what we both helped perpetuate.

-ENDE-

ABOUT THE AUTHOR

Cole Coonce has written about drag racing, drag queens, drum machines, sex machines, ketamine, Kraftwerk, the Land Speed Record, the record business, bicycles, Japanese drifters, high plains drifters, UFOs, quantum mechanics, shade-tree mechanics, famous nobodies that slept on his couch and Mark E. Smith.

He lives in Los Angeles and probably wouldn't live anywhere else.

also available at kerosenebomb.com

INFINITY OVER ZERO (Cole Coonce)

COME DOWN FROM THE HILLS
& MAKE MY BABY (Cole Coonce)

THE INERTIA VARIATIONS (John Tottenham)

ELEPHANT GNOSIS (David Kettle)

DR. BUCKS LETTERS (FallNet)

TOP FUEL WORMHOLE (Cole Coonce)

SEX & TRAVEL & VESTIGES
OF METALLIC FRAGMENTS (Cole Coonce)

www.ingramcontent.com/pod-product-compliance
Lightning Source LLC
Chambersburg PA
CBHW052140170626
46812CB00004B/1516